Leadership Development Step by Step
What makes a successful Leader

O'Neal Johnson Jr.

Copyright © 2020

All Rights Reserved

ISBN:978-1-952263-97-2

"Following is a choice, leadership is a decision."

O'Neal Johnson Jr.

3/8/2021 Tony Newton, thank you for your friendship and counsel. With gratitude and honor.
3 John 2

Dedication

This book is for those who currently lead, develop leaders, and are new aspiring leaders. Thank you for being a leader in your own right. Even if you are new to leadership, it is important to know that, at some point in your life, you have already led, your impact was observed and noticed. We all have the elements and skills to become exceptional leaders! This book is dedicated to all of you.

We have all heard the saying, "you can lead a horse to water, but you can't make it drink." Some leaders would give up! As a laser focused leader, you cannot give up, just add some salt to the oats and they will drink. Leadership is about using your skills and strategies for the best outcome for others!

Acknowledgment

There have been several amazing people who encouraged me during the writing of this book; their support was uplifting.

Starting with my former co-workers from Montgomery County Fire and Rescue Service (MCFRS), especially Oscar Mendez. I would visit his office weekly and state, "I should write a leadership book." and he would reply "Just do it", thank you.

Thank you, Division Chief Charles Bailey for writing the Foreword.

My recruitment "A-team;" Roger Hohman, Matthew Hamner, Ryan Roundtree, Liberty Martin, and Beth Anne Nesselt.

Fire Station 15-C shift that served with me at Burtonsville Volunteer Fire Company. MCFRS Combat Challenge Team Members and MCFRS FEI members.

To my editor, Rachel Dorchak, it all makes sense now, thank you.

The Pikesville Volunteer Fire Company members, thank you.

I also want to thank my church family at Arlington Baptist Church in Maryland, thank you for keeping me grounded. Especially the Arlington family fellowship group.

Sergeants Major USMCR: John Jennings, Randy Neeley and Jerome Alford. Also, the U.S. Marines and sister services members with whom I served with over the years. Especially, LAAD Bn, NWS Earle Marines, 4th CEB, 4th FSSG HQ, HMH772, 838th AEAG Shindand Air Base and 4th CAG.

Thanks for always giving me the straight scoop, Erwyn Lyght, Troy Jones, Johnnie & Dr. Karsonya Whitehead, Kenneth Allen, Michael Hayward, Bryan & Alaina Reese, Joseph & Shloe Jeffery, Jerald & Davelyn James, Bill & Nancy Parsons, John & Alice Harris, John Kelvin Thomas, Tom & Donna Armfield, Jason C. Brezler, Dean Elliott, Larry Murray, Robert I. Ford, D. Eddie Branch, Clarence Voundy, Frantz Pinthiere, Monroe "Butch" Charlton, Mrs. Lillie Green, Rene' Blocker, Donald "Ajax" Rubin, Robert Michael Clemens, Craig Clemens, Brock Cline, Chuck

Earley, Sherry Hohl, Marvin Robinson, Thomas Foster, and Judge Eric Johnson.

The Veterans from the National Montford Point Marine Association, Inc., and my local MD Chapter #17. I especially want to acknowledge The Original Montford Point Marines. I stand on your shoulders, thank you!

Thanks to my fellow Toastmasters, Montgomery County Government Club1510.

To my children: Angelica, Maria, O'Neal III, David, and Joshua, thank you for checking in and giving me feedback at different stages of my book's journey.

To my sisters, Miriam and LaDonna, thank you for all your support over the years.

My mother, Rubye Gilchrist, you have always encouraged and supported me.

Finally, the greatest support and encouragement came from my spouse, Lajuana, you are a super wife and excellent mother to our children. Thank you.

About the Author

O'Neal Johnson Jr. is a retired United States Marine Corps, a Sergeant Major of 30 years, five months, and four days. His experience includes deployments to the Persian Gulf early 80's, South West Asia after the invasion of Iraq into Kuwait (Desert Storm/Desert Shield), Global War on Terrorism, activated after September 11, and the Afghanistan tour after the first surge (Shindand Air Base Command Sgt. Major 2010-2011).

He served as a Captain with the Montgomery County Fire and Rescue Service (MCFRS). He carried out numerous assignments at various fire stations, Station commander at fire station 15, Emergency Communication Center, Fire Explosive Investigation section, assigned as the recruiting manager for MCFRS. Currently, Mr. Johnson Jr. is retired and works in tandem with various organizations, pursuing his passion for philanthropy and driving an enhanced learning skillset.

A New York native who considers 'Baltimore County' home, he graduated from Campbell University in North Carolina with an AA in general studies, moving on to

Columbia Southern University in Alabama, earning a BS in OSHA Safety and minor in Fire Science.

Contents

Dedication .... *i*
Acknowledgment .... *ii*
About the Author .... *v*
Foreword *1*

Chapter 1 - Introduction *4*
    Marine Corps Leadership Principles *8*
    Marine Corps Leadership Traits *9*

Chapter 2 - Setting an Example *13*
    Behavior Orientation *14*
    Pace Establishment *15*
    Communication is the key to several Doors *18*
    Allow each voice to reach your ear *20*
    If you are responsible, then persistently stand responsible *22*
    The Team comes First *26*
    All attention towards you, that is how you maintain coordination .. *27*

Chapter 3 - Leading from the front *30*
    Leading from the back *31*
    Leading from the sidelines *33*
    Leading from the front *35*

Chapter 4 - Counsel *43*
    Short Story *49*

Chapter 5 - Integrity *55*
    Significance of Integrity in Leadership *56*
    Realization of Values and Beliefs *59*
    Impact of Integrity on an Organization *63*
    The Effect on Workers *66*
    Short Story *67*

Chapter 6 - Tolerance *72*
    Mistakes Are How We Learn *73*
    Encouraging Workplace Tolerance *76*

Knowing the Difference between Tolerance and Ignorance 79

Chapter 7 - Mindset 84

Chapter 8 - Consistency 97
    The Key to Success in Long Term Planning 98
    Stability and Growth 101
    Trial and Error 102
    Leaders Can Make Product a Brand – Roadmap to success 103
    Making Sure Everyone is on the Same Page – Actions Speak Louder than Words 105
    Consistency- A Critical Leadership Trait 107
    Consistency in Mood 109
    Consistency in Problem Solving 111
    Consistency in passion for work 112

Chapter 9 - Development 114
    How to build and develop your leadership skills? 117
        Inspire others 120
        Do not close the doors for knowledge 121
        Communicate effectively – Be as clear as possible 122
        Thinking out of the box – The bigger picture 123
        Act before you preach 124
        Helping them discover their strengths 127
        Recognizing their progress 129
        Nurturing their skills 130
        Managing their performance 131

Chapter 10 - The People 133
    As a Leader 136
    You Do Not Build Business, You Build People, Who, Then Build Your Business 137
    Why Do Most of the Sales Leaders Fail to Build Their People? 139
    Customers will never love a company until the employees love it first 143
    What is good people management and what effect does it have? .. 144
    People in Marketing Mix – The 4 P(s) 148
    Problem Solving Is a Major Leadership Quality 151

Chapter 11 - Approachability *156*
  Keeping a "Healthy-Distance" is Not an Effective Leadership Trait
  .... *157*
  An Effective Leader Draws People towards Them; the Leader-Team
  Bond *159*
  Approachability's Pragmatic Leadership Advantages *162*
  Putting the Right People in the Right Places *166*
  Be a Good Listener *168*
  Earning Their Trust *170*
  Reach Out to Them as a Peer or a Friend *171*
  Making Sure Everyone Participates *172*

Chapter 12 - Honesty *174*
  Transparency Is the Key *176*
  What is Honesty? *179*
  What is Integrity? *180*
  What is Trust? *181*
  Do What It Takes *184*
    Model the Path *185*
    Inspire a joint vision and aim *186*
    Takes Challenges and Goes on Ventures *187*
    Inspire others to take the reign in their hands and act *187*
    Encourage people's efforts and appreciate them *187*
    Admitting Their Mistakes *188*
    Powerful Impact of Honesty – Things That Happen When a Leader
    Is Honest *188*

Chapter 13 - Your Mission Is Their Mission *191*
  A Unified Goal *192*
  The Impacts of Unified Direction *194*
  How Do Leaders Work Towards Goal Achievement? *195*
  Make a Vision-Plan *197*
  Make your vision a part of the company's process *198*
  Create a vision from the inside out, not from the top down *200*
  Tie your vision statement with the goals *201*
  Clear and effective communication *202*
  Follow-Ups and Two-Way Feedback *203*

Chapter 14 - Leadership Styles *205*
  Which Type of Leader Are You? *205*

- Autocratic Leadership ... 206
- Democratic Leadership ... 207
- Strategic Leadership ... 208
- Transformational Leadership ... 209
- Team Leadership ... 210
- Cross-Cultural Leadership ... 211
- Facilitative Leadership ... 212
- Laissez-faire Leadership ... 212
- Transactional Leadership ... 213
- Coaching Leadership ... 214
- Charismatic Leadership ... 215
- Visionary Leadership ... 217
- Determine your leadership style - DISC Personality Test ... 220

Chapter 15 - Conclusion ... 222
- Honesty and Integrity ... 224
- Trust Building ... 225
- Commitment ... 226
- Decision Making and Accountability ... 227
- Inspire Others ... 229
- Effective Communication ... 230
- Creativity and Innovation ... 232

Foreword

"Children have never been very good at listening to their elders, but they have never failed to imitate them."
James Baldwin

From the most ancient of days there has been a constant interest in what it means to lead. The clearest evidence of this interest are the many thousands of texts on the subject. Yet, to this day what it means to be a leader is still as opaque as it ever was.

We know it when we see it. When in the presence of good leadership, the signs are clear. The followers are productive; they are united for a common purpose. There is unity and symbiosis. It is evident and clear. Likewise, in the absence of good leadership there is confusion, discontent, and suffering.

It would make sense, then, that so many people would try to capture on paper, which is the ephemeral nature of effective leadership. Leadership must be more than a mere list of qualities and characteristics arranged in a mechanistic, linear way. We all know that leadership is more than a simple adherence to a set of predefined rules. In that way we know easily what it is not, but we struggle a bit more when pressed to explain what it is. When we see effective leadership, we quite naturally emulate the behavior as James Baldwin suggested in the leading quote. However, in study we realize quickly that imitation alone is insufficient. It is insufficient because leadership is also rooted in context. What works in one context can fail in other contexts. It is not a one-size fits all garment.

A collection of individuals is an impotent force only capable of small victories in small contexts. That same group under effective leadership becomes something greater than the sum of the parts. It is in that unity of purpose and action that the presence of leadership becomes most obvious.

One inadequate leader can be more damaging and vicious than Saturn was to his own children. One effective good leader can liberate the vanquished as quickly as Jupiter did for his siblings. And from the absorption of the old lessons the growing leaders of things both small and large, position themselves to be increasingly more effective. In the end the currency that matters most in the exercise of leadership is trust. If when we hear the word leadership, we replace it with the word trust we will not be far off the mark. Trust requires a heart to heart connection between the leader and the led. It requires the intertwining of sinew. As S.L.A Marshall put it in his book Men against Fire: The Problem of Battle Command:

"The heart of the matter is to relate the man to his fellow soldier as he will find him on the field of combat, to condition him to human nature as he will learn to depend on it when the ground offers him no comfort and weapons fail. Only when the human, rather than the material aspects of operation are put uppermost can tactical bodies be conditioned to make the most of their potential unity."

With that in mind, let us continue to study, to absorb points of view that we readily agree with and those with which we take issue. Let us be mindful of our context and let us endeavor to apply the lessons of the past in the hope for a more effective future.

-Division Chief Charles Bailey Montgomery County MD Fire and Rescue Service

Chapter 1
Introduction

We have all heard the saying, "you can lead a horse to water, but you can't make it drink." Some leaders would give up! As a laser focused leader, you cannot give up, just add some salt to the oats and they will drink. Leadership is about using your skills and strategies for the best outcome for others!

A leader is the most essential figure of any organizational structure, as they are someone who translates vision into success. Good leadership sits at the core of any organization's journey of progress and achievement. It is the leadership qualities that define a leader's conduct as well as differentiate him or her from the typical boss behavior, which is proven to be toxic for the organizational structure.

It is essential for a leader to have a clear vision to run an organization by working along with a team of subordinates and associates towards achieving a unified goal. My name is O'Neal Johnson Jr. and I am a retired United States Marine Corps Sergeant Major. I have served a greater part of my life to the U.S. Marines, for 30 years, 5 months and 4 days to be exact, and finally retired at the rank of a Sergeant Major. During my whole life journey until this point, especially during my service period, I have come across a lot of personal life events and experiences, which shaped my mind into thinking toward the importance of leadership development. Moreover, I have gained a lot of exposure from various deployments, which have proven to aid my thinking capacity by broadening my horizons in different dimensions. My experiences include deployments to the Persian Gulf in the early '80s, to Southwest Asia, as well as to Kuwait after the invasion of Iraq (Desert Storm/Desert Shield).

Furthermore, I was mobilized to active duty during the period of Global War on Terrorism (activation after September 11), as well as a tour to Afghanistan (for military purposes) after the first surge (Shindand Air Base Sgt.Maj. 2010-2011).

Currently, I am retired from the Montgomery County Fire and Rescue Service MD (MCFRS). The journey from Marines to present has been exhilarating. The journey has been filled with events and experiences which has made me realize the deeper meaning of life. Although I have learned a lot during this transitional period, I have yet to close the doors of learning new challenges, experiences, and knowledge. A person is never knowledgeable enough.

My emphasis towards learning from the events of life is drawn from my personal experiences. My Marine Corps training and the time that I have served act as sources of learning and education for me. How to behave in real life cannot be taught in classrooms but can be learned through seeking one's behavior through adaptation.

I have mastered numerous assignments by working in different dynamics, even though I stayed in the same field, I have worked at various fire stations, was appointed Station Commander at fire station 15, worked with staff at Emergency Communication center and the Fire Explosive Investigation section and my last assignment was the Recruiting Manager at Montgomery County Fire Rescue Service. Throughout these assignments, I have maintained leadership positions although the dynamics and individuals have changed. I stood standfast in my integrity and character.

I believe my qualities of leadership began with Marine Corps training (boot camp). The Marine Corps has a specific set of rules and regulations that enable a person to be disciplined, well-mannered, well-learned by following some key principles. Although these traits and principles are unheard of or not practiced casually in civil life, upon seeing positive outcomes, I want to make them accessible to the public audience so that they can benefit from them.

I personally believe that every phase of our life is a learning experience, every person we meet, we leave an impact on his or her perception or take an impression from them. If you look back at your life, you will realize the things you have learned in your school life, in turn helped you apply for your first job. Moreover, you will realize that the experiences you gained from your first job must have corrected your conduct towards not repeating the same mistake as you progress in life and apply for another job. Every opportunity that life throws at us, we must grasp onto and try to extract as much knowledge from it as possible.

Marine Corps Leadership Principles

- Know yourself and seek self-improvement
- Be technically and tactically proficient
- Develop a sense of responsibility among your subordinates
- Make sound and timely decisions
- Set the example (serve as an example to your associates)
- Know your Marines (people working with and for you) and look out for their welfare
- Keep your Marines informed
- Seek responsibility and take responsibility for your actions
- Ensure assigned tasks are understood, supervised, and accomplished
- Train your Marines as a team
- Employ your command in accordance with its capabilities

Marine Corps Leadership Traits

- Dependability - The certainty of proper performance of duty

- Bearing - Creating a favorable impression in carriage, appearance, and personal conduct at all times

- Courage - The mental quality that recognizes fear of danger or criticism, but enables a man to proceed in the face of it with calmness and firmness

- Decisiveness - Ability to make decisions promptly and to announce them in a clear, forceful manner

- Endurance - The mental and physical stamina measured by the ability to withstand pain, fatigue, stress, and hardship

- Enthusiasm - The display of sincere interest and exuberance in the performance of duty

- Initiative - Taking action in the absence of orders

- Integrity - Uprightness of character and soundness of moral principles; includes the qualities of truthfulness and honesty

- Judgment - The ability to weigh facts and possible solutions on which to base sound decisions

- Justice - Giving reward and punishment according to the merits of the case in question. The ability to administer a system of rewards and punishments impartially and consistently

- Knowledge - Understanding of a science or an art. The range of one's information, including professional knowledge and an understanding of your Marines

- Tact - The ability to deal with others without creating offense

- Unselfishness - Avoidance of providing for one's own comfort and personal advancement at the expense of others

- Loyalty - The quality of faithfulness to country, the Corps, the unit, to one's seniors, subordinates, and peers

Holding steadfast to the above Marine Corps Leadership Principles and Traits will give you a foundation to resist the war on leadership development.

The British government coined the slogan "Keep Calm and Carry On" in 1939 as the threat of World War II loomed. In the event where Hitler's army invaded England, the posters were to be distributed to England's general population to galvanize their resolve to resist German aggression. Most of us will never have to face that kind of tragedy and adversity in our own lives. Nevertheless, today we find ourselves embroiled in a different kind of war.

That war is Leadership development. Our leadership style seems to be under constant criticism. Our environment has embraced informal leaders, due to which passive aggressive behavior is common in the environment where we lead. When we face leadership conflicts, we must replace the lack of leadership with leadership traits and principles as described in this book. By doing so, our missteps are replaced with confidence and leadership skills, as leadership development has proven to be one of the most influential internal engines to bring change. It sets out to nurture management talent that is entrepreneurial, enterprise-wide, and globally recruited.

I believe this book will provide the readers with a foundational leadership structure. It will provide the energy and inspiration needed to emulate your leadership style. Moreover, I hope this book helps you overcome the challenges you face in any leadership environment.

"Leadership is lifting a person's vision to high sights, the raising of a person's performance to a higher standard, the building of a personality beyond its normal limitations."

Peter Drucker

Chapter 2
Setting an Example

"If there is such a thing as good leadership, it is to give a good example."

Ingvar Kamprad

Every person needs someone to look up to as their inspiration. Someone whom they can learn from. This gives them a ray of hope that they can do better. The feeling of seeing your leader progress can also enlighten you to some tips and tricks on how you yourself can be in that same position.

When you consider someone a leader, you are bound to have some expectations from them. There is a certain set of qualities and skills that you expect from them so that you all have smooth operations in any business. Their most prominent qualities are going to be in the form of advice and resources; they lend you a helping hand. In some rare cases, these leaders involve themselves in your work. Acts like these enable the people associated with the leader to perform better in their fields and increase the productivity of their business. However, there is more to being a leader than simply helping your subordinates. In fact, there is a whole set of criteria that you should set for yourself to be an effective leader. Here in this chapter, you will discover what measures you need to take if you want to become an effective leader and set an example for the people around you.

Behavior Orientation

As the famous philosopher and physician Albert Schweitzer once put it;

"Example is not the main thing in influencing others; it is the only thing."

Having an organized workplace behavior sounds like a significant deal, does it not? Even if it does not matter to you personally, it still matters highly to the leaders who are in charge of a particular workplace. Effective leaders exhibit a behavior that inspires the people around them, rather than alienating them. When you are leading a group of people and they start noticing that they are being kept on the sidelines by you, this is only a recipe for lost loyalty. This is effectively backed up by Tom Landry's theory, which states that leadership is a matter of having people look at you and gaining confidence by seeing how you react. If you are in control, then they are in control. As much as management authorities live in denial about how influential management attributes are, they prove to be an essential factor. in setting an example within the workplace itself. In order to be the standard setter, expecting others to be learning all that you are emanating from yourself, you need to be a learner as well; a pupil who is eager to learn and infuse that learning to all of their followers and peers.

The best part about this learning aspect is that no matter how much information you acquire, there is no harm in getting your hands on more. The more you learn, the better equipped you are at becoming a competent leader. This is because you just slowly work yourself up to the competence level that you are meant to achieve as a leader anyways.

Pace Establishment

Panic is unhealthy when you are leading people. Being paranoid and giving into a freak attack every time someone around you is dealing with a difficult situation is not the right way to go about this. It is a fact put straight that if the leader stresses, the entire pack does. This is simply stated as, the strength of the leader is the strength of the pack. This is the chief lesson taught by Jungle Book. It showed us how we can face the wildest of adversities in the most tactful way possible. Bearing this in mind, you better hold on to those tiny bits of sneak peeks into your childhood memories while you are gearing up for leadership.

Transforming a manageable workload into a drastic nightmare of unwanted stress is nothing but mere foolishness on the part of a leader. An efficient leader will rather sit and invest their time in assessing whether the stress is unreal or existential. This is done so that he or she can set their mind and actions parallel to the situation at hand without further stressing out the people in their vicinity.

Unreal pressure, on the other hand, does not automatically mean that you are not bound to meet deadlines and associate with clients in due time. Unreal or made-to-believe pressure supposedly indicates that you unnecessarily force actions that are not at all needed to fulfil the task at hand. In most cases, pressure or stress that is literally just a piece of your imagination might have you walk out of the door, ignoring all tasks just because there is no urgency to complete them. As far as pace is concerned, rapid, quick, and swift are the kind of put-into-action terminologies that you would seek as a leader. Well-learned leaders know that conflict resolution is a delicate aspect that demands the leader to handle things proactively. If the conflict is taken lightly and not promptly resolved under any circumstances, then it may spark an uncontrolled fire between individuals and teams that might lead to the dissolution of the confidence of the entire pack.

You might assume that it is inevitable for us to encounter arguments or misunderstandings within the workplace, but that is far from the case. Persistent negative approaches between employees should strictly be discouraged. Such behavior does nothing but create hurdles between goals, and that is not what a leader needs to be producing as a communal outcome in the workplace.

Workplace clashes should be openly negotiated and talked about so that a mutual resolution can be achieved at the earliest, thereby preventing one conflict from spreading like an infection and injure the morale of the entire team. It is vital for a leader to bring this into practice to avoid a loss of respect and establish clarity. This also assists with setting up an apt example for other team members to follow.

Communication is the key to several Doors

Strive to sustain healthy and easy-going communication among those working under you. Leaders should guide their subordinates in the right direction. The best way to achieve this purpose is by talking to the people who assist you, exchanging ideas, and by being responsive in maintaining a concrete communication channel. But talking does not mean you just rant without lending an ear to those who tirelessly listen to you.

To receive the input of others, you need to avoid talking and rather initiate a healthy habit of asking. It may not always be productive, but you should ask questions first and make it a point to raise questions, ensuring that they are primarily outcome oriented. Reasonably good questions encourage erudition, clearing the air in case there is a misconception regarding any subject matter, while also continuing to stimulate engagement. Keeping in mind, as previously stated, to act calm and collected during questioning. If you really desire to see these ideas being implemented in your workplace, then you must bring a halt to selfish talking and encourage asking. As substantial as asking and exchanging conversations is, it is just as important to realize their need to be healthy; or at least for them to be delivered in a conventional manner. Words can leave an impact on the people whose ears they enter; for better or for worse. Being a leader in this professional yet sensitive world, one must be a hundred percent alert and conscious of what they utter and to whom. Actions in every situation amplify louder than words, but words can straightaway affect morale and professional productivity; brutally damaging it.

A leader needs to ensure that they exhibit support for the entire team, without alienating any member. It is a leader's job to guide their team members in a detailed manner, so there is no confusion especially if a team member is going the extra mile for the team. You need not hesitate or hold back, you should just make it happen in a way that is most suitable to the work environment and personal satisfaction; that is by offering the necessary guidance behind closed doors. Once you are behind closed doors, there is a reason why it is essential for you to consider how you are going to communicate with others; this particular trait serves as a major facet of great leadership. Since you can never be sure if someone is watching or listening to you, leaders under all circumstances should be mindful of all that they utter and what they put into action. Therefore, talking establishes itself as one of the many ways that allows leaders to set examples in the workplace; but mind you, this must be a cautious exchange of words. Leaders are a prominent figure to the public lens. Therefore, instead of letting the public use this fact in an injurious way, it is better to use this attention in a positive manner to augment yourself as a leader, as well as your assisting staff.

Allow each voice to reach your ear

A leader who negates hearing out and accepting the ideas, suggestions, or concerns from all those involved in a team is never liked by anyone. It is necessary to set an example in this capacity by allowing yourself to be reachable by people who have worries or recommendations to exchange on a serious platform with you. One of the ways to deal with this through an approach that is more accessible is to maintain eye contact and provide proof that you are listening. Furthermore, it would not harm but facilitate your leadership if you ask clarifying questions to ensure that you have developed an understanding of the ideas and are ready to implement a few of them. The 'leader' label usually leads us into being enveloped with the directive approach, where we are prone to command, set orders, and consistently talk. This cuts off the listening factor.

While it is important to provide direction to the team, it is also a key leadership competency to listen to your team and encourage collaboration, giving them your full attention in conversation. Good leadership exhibits a noticeable character that lies in the fact that you acknowledge that you know some things, but not everything.

You need to make it a habit to pay close attention to your team's words and let them settle in your ears and mind, instead of just letting them fall on deaf ears. It is essential that you receive feedback from your team and reciprocate in kind to your team on a regular basis. Promoting the process of listening and encouraging feedback subsequently promotes the team's creativity and makes sure that people in an organization are organized. When you have a recruitment and training engine that is a healthy functioning body, you should definitely look forward to an entire team of experts, since they are a healthy functioning body, maybe they can flex their muscles and generate ideas. Upon asking a question, you will be best served by listening to the response. Listening is an integral part of your professional body behavior, because it does not only allow successful transmission of facts, but it also manages to convey an emotional understanding to your counterpart that you care about their thoughts, their knowledge, and their very presence. Not just for these reasons alone, but for many other ones, you need to learn to listen more as a leader.

If you are responsible, then persistently stand responsible

An efficient and attentive leader always needs to know what they are leading their employees into. Therefore, it is imperative that you establish a vivid vision for the direction of the company, as well as for individual developments. A leader needs to get over the habit of being selfish in a workplace, thinking that it would benefit someone else and not them, because when leadership comes into play, it is very obvious that the benefit from any one member of the team would profit the entire workforce, as well as the organization as a whole. Letting the selfishness alone, the leader needs to exchange their vision with others and display it in front of them; concrete illustrations of what vision casting looks like. Moreover, as the market strategy alters, so does the company's strategic landscape. You must modify your vision as the organization evolves and hence, share a brand-new future for the company to work towards accomplishing.

A leader is to be held accountable for everything that transpires in the workplace, which certainly means that if you or a member on your team happens to make a crucial mistake, as a leader it is your responsibility to take the blame instead of pointing fingers or even allowing anyone to criticize other included members.

Putting the blame on other team members does not only harm the person you are publicly accusing and humiliating in a working environment, but it also paves the way for an unhealthy atmosphere where employees feel scared to ever make a mistake. This in every manner is wrong because it does not just take away a person's liberty to feel comfortable, but it also prevents him or her from learning so they would not repeat the same mistakes. It is crucial that as a leader, you learn to accept blame and strive to bring about remedial resolutions, even if you are personally not at fault. Extraordinary leaders are aware as to when they need to accept mistakes. They take them upon themselves and struggle to solve those mistakes without creating unnecessary drama. Whether you yourself messed up, or your team member did, your approach in fixing the problem should be the same. If you are the leader, you need to take up responsibility for the good, as well as bad, because that is how you maintain an equilibrium in a workplace.

"Managers do things right. Leaders do the right things."

As a leader, part of setting an example is to emit inspiration to the people surrounding you to thrust themselves forward, and in turn be an impetus to the company as it strives for greatness. To do this you must demonstrate the right way by modeling it yourself.

Take a moment to ponder about the inspiring people who have been able to change the landscape of this globe by setting examples for generations to follow. Consider what Mother Teresa accomplished through her actions: for her unwavering commitment to helping those most in need, Mother Teresa stands out as one of the greatest human beings of the 20th century. She combined profound empathy and a fervent commitment to her cause with incredible organizational and managerial skills that allowed her to develop a vast and effective international organization of missionaries to help impoverished citizens across the globe. She was committed in her way, which is why many people continue to follow in her footsteps to date.

Although our situation may greatly differ from Mother Teresa's, the basic principle remains the same. When you lead by example, you are successfully able to erect a picture of what is possible. In such a situation, when you accomplish the canvased picture, people look up to you and develop a belief in themselves, realizing that if you can do it, then they can do it too.

When you lead by example, you carve a pathway that is easy for others to follow. Once you master your leadership skills and offer yourself to your team by demonstrating the way for them, then they will undoubtedly end up following you. When your team is valued, they are loyal and will value you as a leader. Being the leader, if an endeavor fails, you are rightfully meant to be held accountable and answerable. Once you have taken the lead, it is your duty, more than just a goal, to demonstrate your proficiency and expertise in the capacity by giving directions and providing recommendations for people who encounter predicaments in completing their tasks. Nonetheless, you should also encourage the work force to follow concrete steps that you mutually develop, while also intermittently checking back on their progress, considering extra guidance or a change in direction if required.

The Team comes First

Being the leader, you may often be swayed to put yourself and your needs first, but that is the wrong way to go about it. This might seem contradictory, but what it intends to convey is that you are not supposed to devalue any of your team members, no matter what the circumstances may be. Throwing team members under the bus by taking ownership of everything that may be happening, is straightaway harsh and wrong on every level. When you consider putting your team first, this propagates loyalty among the members. It is essential that you share a conversation with your team to learn what they desire and eventually draft out meaningful incentives. Spare indispensable time to accompany team members who are struggling through a personal or professional dilemma, so that you consider their situation too and then decide on a solution that facilitates everyone in a beneficial manner.

For what matters the most is that you need to know how to implement the leadership authority that you possess. While managing them, you should not end up micromanaging them. You are ideally supposed to convey and debate over the mission, vision, and goal. Subsequently, a different goal to master is the ability to step back and allow the team to function, while using what has been provided to them. Setting this example for the people who are following you will encourage other potential managers on your team to apply the same moves.

All attention towards you, that is how you maintain coordination

One of the most effective ways to demand attention is to refrain from trivial collaborations. It is certain that when your team respects you, their attention will be all yours whenever you wish to converse with them, and they will aptly respond in kind. Although there are many different leadership styles you can employ, it is important that you act as a leader and not as a friend to your employees. If you constantly allow yourself to appear friendly toward your employees, people will find it hard to invest trust in your vision. Moreover, putting disciplinary obligations into play and allowing criticism to apply to your peers becomes way too tough when you are not the established leader of the company. This happens because people in a workplace believe what they see, and they need to visualize you as the leader to follow you as one.

It is highly possible that you became a leader by accident, but accidents are also a predestined act of your fate. Maybe you just happened to be that one person who knew how to develop a mind-blowing android application; one that no one else could, and that is how your coincidental talent turned out into a miracle of fate.

When leaders prioritize career advancement prospects, they exhibit their commitment to the welfare of their team. Another important aspect of leadership responsibility is being able to support your workers by technically polishing their skills. To bring out the best in your teammates and to encourage them to take up more responsibilities in the near future, you need to comprehend their objectives and encourage innovation within them.

Empowering people who are following your directions is not an impossible task. In fact, leaders remain in a position to aid their team members' professional development. Professional development is an extraordinary mechanism for facilitating growth. However, as a leader, you must demonstrate your commitment towards the expansion of your team's reach by highlighting augmentation prospects. It is also necessary that you occasionally put yourself and your team to the test.

When collaborating, you both are better able to overcome your shortcomings by working together. Once professional development seems to be an aspect well-established and accomplished, you must acknowledge and reward proactive participation to build enthusiasm and encourage continued progress.

Chapter 3
Leading from the front

"People ask the difference between a leader and a boss. The leader works in the open, and the boss in covert. The leader leads, and the boss drives."

Theodore Roosevelt

There is a difference between being a boss and being a leader. Leading as a boss means that you are controlling and directing people's actions, but not engaging in the activity yourself, whereas being a leader puts you as a member of the group working towards a common vision. That is what most effective leaders do because they know that vision matters and that once you have a vision, there is no need left to question why it matters or not.

This statement is more of a reflective statement for the people out there trying to be leaders. It is important to take a pause and consider whether you are leading from the front or leading from behind, and what is more useful to you. Are you pushing and directing people to do something that they are not committed to; are you seeking people out to come work towards and to come work towards a prospective vision? I am sure you have probably heard of the saying 'Lead by example'. Well this is what it means, leading from the front where you can set an example. If whatever it is that you are doing is able to inspire others to be a part of it and work for it, then you are indeed a leader and you have been successful at setting an example. There are various leadership styles that one can see being used and embraced. But in this chapter, we are going to be focusing on the most effective one, leading from the front. However, I think it is important to take a brief look at the other leading styles before delving into what leading from the front entails.

Leading from the back

Leading from the back is more of a check and balance style of leadership that drives the team forward to gain momentum. Of course, all leaders need to know this type of leadership as well because it is a given that in their career, they will not always be leading from the front. Even if it is the style that they prefer. Leading from the back is sort of a risky process because it can mean a few things for different people and only the right meaning will actually allow them to move forward. One of the general perceptions about this style of leadership is that the leader, instead of accomplishing the goals, will instead rest the completion of the goals on the shoulders of their team. or forces the team to complete the goals needed to accomplish the mission without the leader. It is easy to see how that misconception can end up making the team become counterproductive, harbor ill feelings, and create discord among team members.

However, the essence of leading from behind is that the leaders move out of the way and lets the team members take over so that real growth can take place. That is the only way that leading from behind can lead to organic growth, without any negative misconceptions. However, it can be tricky to achieve and the time it takes to clear away other perceptions may render this type of leadership style ineffective.

The good leaders in this case are the ones who could build teams that can operate on their own in almost any environment. It is often hard for leaders to let go of control of their team after a certain point and then allow them to sink or swim based on their actions alone. The parent instinct kicks in and naturally so because it is built upon the same concept. The greatest parents are those that raise their children in a way that they can survive and operate independently. The parents are going to be there of course, but the children do not always need them because they are self-sufficient and can sustain themselves. At that point, it becomes hard for a parent to watch their children sink or swim based upon what they do because they feel obliged to step in to help because they feel responsible. Of course, there is a lesson to learn here. If the goal is to build a team of individuals that can be autonomous, problem solving or adaptive as necessary, to find situations on their own, then the eagles must be made to leave the nest.

Leading from the sidelines

This type of leadership involves the leaders acting more like coaches in a democratic leadership style to ensure that everyone is moving forward together in the same direction. Leading from the sidelines is sort of a transitional style of leading that takes into account the questions of whether a leader should just go ahead and do something themselves and set that expectation, or wait to get everyone on board and provide assistance. You see, delegation is one of the most difficult tasks for a leader and so, if you want it done right, do it yourself" Leaders need to change their concept of the right way and allow others to complete the task in his or her way. However, every time something comes up all the other team members are left wondering whether the leader will do it first so that they can follow. This ends up creating a bottleneck for the productivity schedule, because the people are just waiting for the leader to complete the task, take over, fulfill the request/duty/goal.

To overcome this bottleneck, leading from the sidelines became the preferred leading style, where leaders can move out of the way and let their team member's move forward but not be completely out of the picture. Instead, they will be moving with the team on the sidelines, ready to help where needed. The drawback that some leaders might find in this is that when the team rises or falls, the leader will have to remain on the sideline. This means that the extent of their assistance capabilities is limited. The underlying principle in this leading style is that the team members should be given the freedom to make their own mistakes as well, but that does not mean that the leader is not present for assistance and support.

Leading from the front

This brings us to the focus of this chapter; leading from the front where the leader sets the pace, destination, and direction for his team members. This simply means that a leader is demonstrating his or her leadership by going first and setting an example. In a lot of cases, this is accomplished when the leader completes the most difficult tasks first, ensuring confidence in the vision for the team.

This confidence can manifest in a positive beginning mindset. Telling people what to do is different from the leader showing or demonstrating what needs to be accomplished and completed. Telling someone means you are giving out orders or directing a group of people. It may work out well in the sense that if the people are highly motivated, then they will find a way to do the task and they will end up learning a lot.

But when a leader does it himself or herself, then the motivation of the team is automatically raised and what seemed daunting or impossible before now seems attainable. Anything can seem attainable when you personally know someone who has done it. Think of something that you have been unsure about doing, but you found out that one of your friends did it. Take skydiving for example. It can be pretty much a nightmare for some people. But of course, some people are highly motivated to go through it alone whereas others need someone else to encourage them to do it. Imagine that one of your friends skydives and has been through its numerous times. If he or she guides you through the process, then it will be much easier for you because the person assisting you is someone you know and trust. You can ask them for advice resulting in a successful skydiving activity!

Therefore, leaders need to think of the impact that they can have if the team members see that they are willing to do the small stuff as well. For example, can you think of a time when your boss or someone else's boss wrote their own Christmas card? What would be the general perception if they did? Was it them stooping down to the level of the other employees, or does it say something about the character of a leader? That is the type of behavior that has the power to motivate on a more permanent basis. That is the behavior that lets people know that it's the little things that count – and that success is within reach.

How often do we see leaders, not real leaders, tell followers to do things they themselves would not do? Many real leaders do not believe in asking their team to do anything they themselves would not do. An attitude such as this can often mean a great deal to team members. However, it can also at times be unrealistic. I have seen a lot of leaders in my career, and when I think back to all of the times that I saw those leaders right in the middle of everything, working alongside the rest of us, I realized that most of them were ineffective leaders. The thing was that most of them were the ones who were there working with the rest of the team members because they were comfortable in doing the work, rather than leading the process.

It was then that I learned that there was a difference between leading by setting an example, and leading by working, because that is your comfort zone. The people who are leading because they are comfortable working alongside everyone else are not actually leaders, but instead managers. They believe their role consists of managing people and the workload, which is why they choose that position from where they can manage the team members easily. These are the kind of people who tend to get lost in the nitty gritty details. Since one of the qualities is micromanaging, managers tend to have difficulty seeing the big picture unlike leaders who allow their team to complete the small details to build the bigger picture. A leader can only provide direction when he or she can see the bigger picture or the end goal, but if that is not the case then there is no point in working so hard and losing sight of the destination.

It is a common business term to come across, but it is not always effective because making it effective is an art. We have heard this phrase before, especially for business students, but there is a need to shift the perspective from 'do as I do' to 'I am willing to do whatever it is I am telling you to do'. The two may seem similar concepts, but the second definition of leading from the front has several differences from the first. The first error in the 'do as I do' model is that most leaders fail to realize that in a lot of cases, there will be employees or workers that will not be willing to do what the leaders are doing. You have to take into consideration that an average employee may feel that a certain level of success is out of their reach, or they may not be willing to put in the required amount of effort to get there.

One major difference between a manager and a leader is that while a manager believes that their job is to manage people, a leader believes that his or her job is to manage the process of the people and help them to grow. When a person is up front and engaged in doing the daily work, they simply cannot establish the perspective necessary to see the process in its entirety. Therefore, they miss the opportunity to develop their people.

This now implies that leading from the front is not as simple as just getting to work alongside your team and setting an example, because even managers can do that. It means that leading from the front should mean being visible at the front while still being able to see the destination from amongst the obstacles and guiding your team. Guiding your team from the front means you are equally involved in all of the risks.

As a leader, it is not entirely possible to be at the front of all processes and tasks where you can work equally as much as your team members. But what you can do is take up responsibility from the front and see the broader perspective. Empowering the people to do the work is the correct approach here. From the front, you can see the moving parts of your team where they will be exposed to danger or risk and where they can play on their strength. You can also see the obstacles before your team encounters them and so you can come up with damage control strategies or ways to avoid them. Effective leaders that lead from the front are the ones that remain engaged in all levels of the process but will be somewhat disengaged from the details. By empowering people who do the work, leaders grant the decision-making to the team members since they know all of the details of the work, since they are the ones close up with the details of the work. Front line leaders also let the front-line workers plan the strategies and execute processes to groom and develop them as future leaders. This way, they stay close enough to coach but far enough to see all the field of work and what might be coming up ahead. It is pretty much impossible to guide the workers if you are too far away from your team's frontline.

I think you can see for yourself now that leading from the front does not mean that the leader runs ahead. In fact, it means whoever is first, knows the steps needed to accomplish the goal, while the leader is standing at a vantage point where he or she can gauge any oncoming barriers. The front is a matter of perspective. Many people assume that it means the front of the working line, whereas it means being even further. Being a good front leader means that you understand what perspective you need to take to ensure that the bigger mission is accomplished. Truly leading from the front does not necessarily mean that leaders must be involved in doing heroic acts and hold bragging sessions. The team members will know that the leader cares about them because he or she is never going to ask them to do something that they themselves would not do.

We talk about leading from the front from an entirely different perspective, more specifically as a team leader in a creative firm. Only a leader who holds themselves responsible on behalf of their team possesses the ability to lead their team from the front during the different crucial phases. When their team is having trouble dealing with deadlines, it is the responsibility of their leader to work overtime, come up with a strategy and be patient to prevent themselves and their entire team from collapsing and facing severe drawbacks.

Vision is the main tool leaders use to lead from the front. Effective leaders do not push or provoke their followers. They do not boss them around or manipulate them. They are in the front, showing the way. The vision allows leaders to inspire, attract, align, and energize their followers—to empower them by encouraging them to become part of a common enterprise dedicated to achieving the vision.

Chapter 4
Counsel

"A leader must be a good listener. He must be willing to take counsel. He must show a genuine concern and love for those under his stewardship."

James E. Faust

Being a great leader is not an easy job. With great power comes great responsibilities. If you want to be a leader, there are plenty of aspects that need to be managed/ supervised and followed consistently to have a positive turnout in the end. Out of those many aspects that make a great leader, one is '*counseling*', which is an important factor to remember. With all of that aside, here we are going to be focusing on '*counseling*', which is mandatory for a leader. Why? Well, the mentoring and coaching of their subordinates may be a good factor but counseling them is entirely different. Counselling solely focuses on the subordinates' betterment and how they can improvise in their field. When a leader counsels their subordinates, he or she is preparing another leader to take his seat when he or she retires. One major problem that some leaders get often confused about is that they think this might create competition for them and their subordinates will eventually replace them well before the right time comes.

This is actually a misconception, which restrains numerous leaders from fully focusing on their subordinates as they do not want to lose their designation in the firm they have been serving for so long. Leaders need to understand that counseling their subordinates, or even other people working under them, will only ease their burden and their work-load. Dividing this workload can result in a much easier job for all individuals involved. The firm will not be dependent on just a bunch of people during a critical phase if the rest of the teams are strong enough to play their part and perform up to their full potential.

Before proceeding any further, we must remember that a leader only counsels the people working under them once he or she feels empathy towards them. This is because it focuses only on the betterment of the people being counseled. Consider it as a sort of leverage the person being counseled receives. I am stating this because there is always at least more than one person being supervised by the leader, and not all of them get to be counseled by the leader. There may be mentorship programs, or even training programs, for them to take a step ahead in the firm, but counseling is entirely different. Besides, almost every great personality in this world was mentored, trained, and counseled at one point to reach their fame. Take Arnold Schwarzenegger as an example. He is globally famous for being a great athlete and a world-class actor as well.

We all have heard his story of how he ran from the military to pursue his passion for being a bodybuilder, which later resulted in him getting opportunities to model, and he ended up becoming an actor. But how was he able to do it? Was he able to achieve it all alone? Not. There was always someone to lead him, to guide him, to be his mentor and to counsel him.

Even though he is one of the greatest personalities to ever exist on this planet earth, there was someone who was better than him who guided him towards the best path. It goes without saying that his mentors or teachers must have changed during his lifetime as the phases changed. For instance, his teacher or mentor would have been somebody else when he was an athlete and chose to be a bodybuilder.

The teacher or mentor would have changed automatically when he switched to being a fashion model and then again when he opted to be an actor. All of them were experts in their own fields and helped Arnold groom himself for a better future without being concerned. One person would not have been able to do it on their own. All of them must have passed on some important lessons to Arnold during his journey, which would have helped him in shaping his future for the better. But not even one of them could have stuck around with him throughout.

Let us not get confused here, people often wonder if a person may only lead an entire team to be a leader. Well, training an individual and helping them become leaders makes them a better person. This is because the word 'leader' itself means to lead towards the right path, in the right direction. It does not emphasize anywhere that the leader is supposed to lead an entire fleet to be recognized for his qualities and skills. It varies from profession to profession, and from experience to experience. A new leader may have the ability to lead a bunch of people and bring out their full potential for their performance but may face a harsh time when asked to lead a group of different people. It can be due to a lack of experience. Talking about experience, speaking as a leader to a leader, do not be worried when you are assigned to handle and lead a team of people who are not organized. It may seem like one hell of a mess, but that task is not impossible at all. Do not be afraid to take on that challenge of leading the troubled team. If you have even the slightest doubt of failure, tackle it. What is the worst that can happen? A mere goal or objective will not be accomplished by the end of the day or by the end of an entire week, that is just how it is.

It will not be the end of the world. Be optimistic at this stage now. You are going to gain experience and, you are going to learn from that experience. Nothing will be lost as you will only gain. That, too, depends on how you see it. If you look at that phase as a bad phase of your life that is going to leave a bad impression on you, then you may be in trouble. Remember, always seek out a mentor.

Note to self, remember that people only look at the success of others, but often undervalue the struggles that they needed to overcome to succeed. If I ever find myself stuck in a situation where I may not be performing up to my full potential, I move forward and attempt to forget the ordeal, considering it a bad dream. Of course, my perspective may be a lot different than yours and my way of getting over things may be different or a little absurd. But you get the idea. Do not let the negative energy take over you and drain you. Try and learn from it. There is a high possibility that you are going to face a much more demanding and challenging situation in the future, so you better learn from it, straighten up your shoulders and face those challenges head on. It may become one of your biggest fears and restrain you from progressing in the future. You may miss out on several opportunities because of this, and that is certainly not healthy for your personal development. A setback or failure paves the roadway for a comeback!

So far, we have understood why counseling is an essential aspect for a leader to look after. Now we shall focus on an aspect that is of great importance to a leader, responsibility for the wellbeing of his or her subordinates. If a leader succeeds in fulfilling his or her duty, they will have less workload while also having the time to counsel and groom their staff. Counseling can be a difficult task and an even more difficult thing to explain. The following short story will focus on counseling as a leader in a real work scenario to help make this task clearer.

Short Story

Struggling and hustling on the streets of New York, Danny was just an ordinary stockbroker trying to chase and live the American dream, just like every other corporate slave walking on the same street. Having started his own family a couple of years back, his marriage was not working out as expected, which was a problematic phase for him to deal with. Continually struggling every day to achieve his daily target by the end of the day, was putting so much stress on him that the harder he was trying to work the more he was pushing himself to the verge of breaking down.

In addition to his miserable fortune, Danny soon got fired from his job over a dispute concerning being involved in a brawl with his fellow co-worker. The loss of a job resulted in the end of his marriage as well. Now, Danny was just a mere guy sitting on the couch, binge-watching television shows, and imagining having a good time as it was the only thing that could comfort him and keep him away from the harsh reality. As the time went by, Danny was losing cash quickly and there was no source of income for his survival. Danny started searching for different jobs to support himself, but the odds were not in his favor. He once dreamed of having all the luxuries in life, like everyone else, but the chances of his dream coming to life were now minimal.

There was no motivation left in Danny and he was losing hope, until one day he came across an advertisement of '*Stockbroker – Wanted*'. The only catch was that it was from a small firm. At first, Danny thought it would be a waste of his time, but then he realized that something is better than nothing for the sake of his survival. He picked himself up and went for the interview.

Looking at his experience and skill set, and at the fact that the firm was a start-up, Danny got hired for a fair salary immediately. It was quite an achievement for Danny that he was employed once again after such a decline in his life and three months of unemployment. His hopes were now being restored and he was yet again determined to give it a shot and risk it all for his dreams. Being successful in the new firm and flooding them with profits soon led to his promotion as a manager of a team of stockbrokers. This promotion worked as a motivation booster for Danny and now his goals seemed much easier to achieve. Month after month, Danny was climbing his way to the top. He was being rewarded by the firm for growing at a faster pace and he was also adding more stuff to his personal wish list. One of the best aspects of his job was his mentor, his leader. Even though Danny was a manager, his supervisor was still focused on him, training him to be a better team player. It was evident that the mentorship of his leader was going to benefit him in the long run. Danny was continually being taught to share what he had learned with his team; he showed them how to handle stressful situations.

Sooner than expected, Danny felt like it was time to go solo. He resigned from the firm on good terms and started his own company. It was a company with no boundaries, and no restrictions. The better the performance of the employee, the more rewards they got. His new strategy seemed attractive and the firm started off smoothly. Danny's approach was slightly different, but it was boosting the motivation level of his employees. Being the CEO of the company, he had to wisely choose people for executive designations. During his time at the previous firm, he had built up enough contacts that he was able to hire a team of dedicated and determined executives to look after his firm. Despite being at the highest possible rank of his firm, he still chose to involve himself with the managers and executives of his firm to share his experiences and give out tips and lessons on how to stay focused. Out of the entire fleet of executives and managers, there was one manager who appeared more enthusiastic than the rest. He was more of his reflection during his struggles.

When Danny looked at his exotic car parked near the port, close to his yacht, he felt the urge that he should do something to groom himself so he can grow into something big. That is when Danny remembered the lessons taught to him by his mentor in the previous firm, and he began implementing the same strategies on himself.

Danny promoted him from the managerial post to his subordinate and started counseling him because he wanted him to be better than the rest at the firm. This was the difference between him and other managers and executives of Danny's firm. The outcomes of Danny's efforts were evidently positive, and the subordinate was doing an amazing job in leading the entire team of executives and managers towards achieving their goals with ease. Danny realized that he took the right opportunity to invest his time in his subordinate. Danny's business was being driven smoothly and they were able to cash in more new businesses than before. Danny decided to introduce a new policy of high-end rewards for employees who perform up to their full potential. This step was taken to reward his subordinate with the luxuries that he deserved, but it would seem unfair to other employees if he would have just started giving out expensive rewards to those he liked, regardless of how justified his preferences were.

To make everything appear professional, Danny promoted his subordinate to the designation of CFO and then started monitoring everyone's performance. To make it fair, he gave out rewards to those employees who were good performers as well, but the CFO of the company received the keys to a brand new exotic car for his relentless efforts of 4 months as a CFO in making the company reach the top. The reward was widely appreciated by the entire firm and it urged other employees to work even harder as well. The hard work and dedication of the employees were surely beneficial to them, but on the other hand, Danny was the one who was getting closer and closer to achieving his American dream.

Within three years after the launch of his firm, Danny was now sitting on the pinnacle of success. His skills to lead different teams, motivate employees, mentor, and invest in his firm set an example for the newly recruited employees.

Danny's story perfectly described how a leader should prioritize counseling his or her subordinate and how it can benefit the leader in the long run. Investing time and efforts in the subordinate is an investment in oneself.

Now that our concept regarding counseling has been clarified, we can now proceed to the next topic that emphasizes *'integrity'*. By the end of this book, the goal is to ensure that the readers have clearly understood every aspect and factor of this book so they can implement it in their lives. Implementation of the lessons learned will result in having a step ahead in life and decrease the chances of making mistakes. Indeed, making mistakes teaches some of the best lessons, but not always. Some mistakes can be avoided if the leader is well informed on the key aspects needed to lead. All of the efforts and progress goes down the drain and you will not be able to achieve what you were aiming for, like Danny.

Chapter 5
Integrity

"The supreme quality for leadership is unquestionably integrity. Without it, no real success is possible, no matter whether it is on a section gang, a football field, in an army, or in an office."

Dwight D. Eisenhower

For many years now, not only researchers but several managers and supervisors have proposed several ways to lead a certain group of workers. Various approaches toward leadership specifically in a workplace have been shared in the past. However, one thing that is always found in all these theories related to effective leadership is the element of integrity. One of the most essential qualities of a successful leader is the integrity in their nature. A leader is the person who shows the right path to a group of people and guides them to their destination. To do so, it is necessary that first the leader has a clear vision of that path. A leader is only able to tell the difference between what is right and what is not with their quality of integrity.

When you hear the word integrity what comes to your mind? A sense of responsibility? Feeling accountable? Or loyalty? Well the concept of integrity is more related to loyalty. It basically refers to the traits of honesty and truthfulness. This is the quality that every good person possesses, an individual who people can place their trust in, whether he is a leader or an acquaintance. In the previous chapters, we discussed the responsibilities and traits of an effective leader. Now we will focus on the integrity of a leader and how this affects the performance of the workers. Not only that, but we will also see the ways in which this characteristic of a leader can completely change the culture of an organization.

Significance of Integrity in Leadership

It is human to be true and faithful in his or her dealings and actions. When a person does something wrong or maintains a deceiving attitude, initially it might seem like they are lying or being dishonest to ensure their personal gain or advantage. However, in the back of their mind, they will always have a bad feeling for making such decisions as he goes completely opposite to their nature. Similarly, the individuals in a group always want to do the right thing. Having an honest leader who is true in his trades and follows all the codes of ethics, gives the followers an assurance that they will always stick to the right path and even if they stray from it, their leader will bring them back to righteousness.

It might seem like just a simple word "Integrity" however, it has a very deeper meaning to it and can be considered as the combination of numerous qualities that a leader should hold within them. When a leader is consistent in their techniques, ethics, beliefs, activities and can deliver the same results, this shows that they may encapsulate the quality of integrity in their nature. This teaches the leader to always side with whatever is the right thing to do.

The honesty in a frontrunner's nature always compels them to make the best decisions no matter the situation. Since many people's fate relies on the leader's decisions, it is extremely crucial that a leader is proficient in their judgement and always decides to do the right thing so that truthfulness could prevail at a larger level. Therefore, it can be established that the crux behind the concept of integrity is to choose right from wrong.

When you lead a few people, it is important for you to maintain discipline, otherwise you will prove to be an inefficient leader. Either you are leading a group of workers or social activists, the individuals of that team will only follow you and take your advice when they see you working by the code of conduct. A leader is a person who inspires the people and gives constant vibes of positivity to their subordinates.

When there is an absence of integrity in them, it can be difficult for a leader to show his good side to the people who look up to him. People will always doubt his judgement and get a skeptical feeling in following his instructions as by observing his character, they would notice a significant lack of reliability. This is also one of the major reasons why a leader needs to work on their integrity and needs to make sure that their actions and ideas show the goodness that they hold inside of them.

There are many traits that a leader can miss out on and still manage to effectively meet his objectives and targets. However, integrity would significantly lessen a leader's effectiveness. When a moment of crisis arises, it is the leader who makes the quick decisions and guides the people on how to handle such a situation. For instance, if the fire department gets a call in the middle of the night, it is an old lady who needs help and is unable to provide the required information. She specifies that there is no fire in the house, but she fell and cannot get up. Now a captain who lacks integrity would tell the lady that she needs to call an ambulance or that they would direct her to another social services department who can help her. However, an honest captain will not make the lady go through any further trouble and would just probe efficiently to get the needed information. Then he would respond with an ambulance or fire apparatus to assist and rescue that poor lady. That is the importance of integrity in a leader and this how a leader sets an example for his followers.

Realization of Values and Beliefs

Factually speaking, a leader shapes the culture of an organization. The people who work under supervision, their loyalty to the company, and respect for the company's policy also relies on the beliefs and values of their supervisor. The way a leader looks toward the decisions made by the higher management forms the perceptions of the individuals who work under them. It is true that the managers are the ones who set the direction in which an organization moves. Specifically, if you talk about the armed services like the Army or the Marines, the recruits blindly follow the orders of the commander as they are trained this way. Therefore, it is important for the commander to understand that his beliefs and values set an example for his troops to follow.

It is vital for the beliefs and values of a leader to reflect integrity in them. Several CEOs and employees of different companies seem to believe that in an organization the element of trust is the thing, which transforms a random manager into a remembered leader. Successful leadership is all about gaining the trust of subordinates so that you can trust in them to get the job done.

A supervisor is only able to gain the trust of his workers when he holds true to his promises that he makes to them. If a worker approaches the manager with a concern and then the manager assures the employee that the issue will be resolved, then the matter should be concluded long before the employee feels the need of mentioning the problem to the manager once again. This gives the idea to the employees that they can place their faith in their leader and not worry about the matter being resolved once they have shared their affairs with the manager. The trait of integrity is prominently observed in the actions of the leader when he shows loyalty to his followers. Similarly, there are numerous ways in which a leader can make sure that he has honest values and beliefs or can make sure that honesty is at the center of their value and beliefs. It is particularly important for the success of an organization that the employees have a good relationship with their manager.

For any kind of relationship to succeed, trust is the most important factor that should exist between people. Other than that, a leader needs to be very fair in making decisions. We have already established that a good leader is always able to differentiate between right and wrong. Therefore, before he takes any step, he should carefully analyze the situation and then then choose a decision that seems right and just.

For instance, there is a specific criterion which the students need to meet to pass the exam. A teacher decides to fail a student as the student's performance seemed to be consistently poor. However, the principal overrules the judgement of the teacher and instructs the teacher to pass the student. Later, the teacher gets to know that the student was the son of one of the primary trustees of the school which is why the principal decided to pass the student. Now, the teacher will never trust the judgement of the principal and will consider him to be unworthy of being the head of the school. The principal will lose all his credibility in front of the teacher, and the teacher will always feel uncomfortable working under the supervision of such a headmaster.

In addition to that, to achieve effective leadership, it is imperative for the leader to acknowledge the achievements of his followers and appreciate them. If we specifically talk about a mission being accomplished, it is true that the decision making and providing the appropriate guidance to the troop was the commander's doing. However, the final act was indeed performed by the troops who acted upon his orders. Therefore, the commander should not take all the credit for the success in the assignment as it was a team effort, and every member of the team had the same level of contribution in the mission. It is often observed that managers try to take credit for the work that is done by their subordinates. Adopting such values and beliefs gives an impression to the followers that their leader severely lacks integrity in him and that it will always be a disadvantage for them to work under the shadow of such a leader.

Impact of Integrity on an Organization

Any organization, whether it belongs to the corporate world or provides social services to the public, looks for an individual who can differentiate between right and wrong and has the strength to do what is right. Specifically, when a person is hired for the position of a manager or a supervisor, the company ensures that the individual comprises the trait of integrity in them.

How does a company ensure this when a person is being hired? Is it an interview question or past experience? When a person is honest it is more likely that they will prioritize company policy and follow the business's rules and regulations. This honesty will inspire other individuals working under the leader to follow the same moral guidelines. This would help an organization develop a positive culture at the workplace and enhance the performance of the human resource. As discussed previously, a leader always bears a great deal of responsibility on their shoulders. Once a person is promoted to a leadership position in a company, it is important that they are cautious about moral judgements. Companies value that person the most who shows that they really care about rules and is also concerned about the ethical behavior of the people around them. Many professionals from the corporate world believe that the leaders who value integrity are a great asset to the organization.

Tim Hird is a well-known professional in the corporate world. These are his thoughts about the impact of integrity in a leader's character on the business of a company, *"Companies with strong, ethical management teams enhance their ability to attract investors, customers and talented professionals"*. It can be considered as a complete chain of actions.

The company first needs to ensure that the people who sit in high management positions value the element of honesty, so that while selecting the manager for the operations. Change starts from the top as the person who falls in the lowest level of hierarchy in a company always follows the footsteps of higher authorities. When the followers see the leader caring for the right thing and honoring the profitability of the organization, the employees are most likely to adopt the same practices. As a result, an overall change is observed in the environment of the organization, which not only seems to satisfy the stakeholders of the business but also attracts new professionals who value ethics.

Considering these factors, leaders need to realize that they are the individual who is shaping the culture and true values of the company. The decisions they make, the management techniques they use, and their actions define the culture of the organization. In the start of this chapter, we learned that managers need to build the trust of their subordinates to work with them effectively.

When a leader understands that their followers determine the effectiveness of their decisions based on their integrity, then they will automatically try to treat his followers in the best possible manner. This will not only create a good relationship between the managers, but it will also bring a positive change in the workplace where the workers and supervisors both respect each other's judgement and opinions.

The Effect on Workers

We have already talked a lot about how an employee determines the character of his leader. Now let us discuss in a bit more detail how workers are affected by the integrity of their leader. When an employee can believe that his manager is trustworthy, and they would follow his instruction without question. Only the honesty of a leader can lead the subordinates to build up such a kind of faith in the manager. The reason why I have been emphasizing positive relationships between the manager and the subordinates is because it has a significant impact on the business.

When the subordinates can rely on their managers, they do not hesitate in approaching the manager for an issue at any point of time. This way they can minimize the errors in their work and are able to produce quality outcomes in a shorter time. The organization also gains a chance of maximizing their profits as the efficiency of their workforce increases. It is often observed that the employees associate the acts of kindness and positive intentions of an individual with his/her integrity. They might be right to do so to some extent as the things that a person wants to accomplish tell a lot about the character of that person.

Similarly, a person who is fair and always prefers to do right by every individual that comes across him, he will always want to talk kindly and be nice with the people around him. When a leader, through his actions, demonstrates some inappropriate intentions that may pose a threat to the organization as well, then this can lead to two different outcomes. outcomes in a shorter time in either case, the organization faces some fatal disadvantages. The following short story will encapsulate the importance of integrity in a leader and will give you a clearer picture of how it impacts the organization and its workers.

Short Story

John was a regular employee of the superstore and worked as a cashier there. He was a bright young fellow who was exceptionally soft spoken and kind by nature. Everyone knew him because of his friendly attitude and his ability to get along with almost every single person who worked at the store. He had only worked for a few months when the management decided to promote him to the post of store manager. His skills and competencies made him worthy of the designation as he was already quite efficient in doing his work. Even though he was on good terms with every other employee of the mart, as soon as he got promoted, the behavior of a few other workers started to change toward him. They had worked at the store way longer than John had, this was also the reason why they started to envy him, however John tried his best to give a neutral treatment to all of the workers once he became the manager.

One day a lady came to the store for groceries. She had bought a lot of stuff from the store. She was a frequent customer and was usually seen shopping at the store where John worked. However, this time she was so involved in handling all the stuff that she had bought, that she forgot her handbag on the payment counter. The cashier who cleared her bill was Patrick.

He was the one who found her handbag but did not immediately inform the management about this as a few negative thoughts started entering his mind. Everyone knew that John was very vigilant about the rules and regulations and always opted for the right thing to do, even the cashier knew this about John. Patrick noticed the handbag and quickly hid it from view, planning to go through the contents when he was finished with his shift. However, the cashier on the next counter noticed this activity of Patrick and quietly approached John to inform him about the incident. The way John handled this situation determined his true potential as a manager of the store. John did not react in any rash manner nor did he lash out on Patrick for such an act. He simply called Patrick to his office and had a normal conversation about what had happened. John did not let Patrick know that another employee had informed him about Patrick stealing a customer's handbag, instead he said that he had received a call from the customer inquiring if they had found a handbag. At first, Patrick consistently denied that he knew anything about the handbag.

However, after constant probing, Patrick confessed to John that he had indeed hid the handbag. To support his actions, Patrick told John that the store policy and several signs in the store clearly stated that the customers need to care for their stuff on their own and that the store will not be responsible for any such loss. Patrick was also one of those people who were jealous of the promotion that John had earned. Considering that John was a little inexperienced and younger than Patrick, he was planning to pin the whole incident on John. However, John was also very clever. As soon as Patrick started to tell him about what he had found in the handbag and that they could split the money and no one would have to know, John was smart enough to see where Patrick was going with this. The honesty that resided within John gave him the courage to forgo his own personal benefit in the best interest of his customer. He did not even take one second to deny the offer that Patrick had made and instantly gave him a warning that he can lose his job and credibility in the store if he does not turn in the handbag with complete belongings of the customer that were inside it.

The seriousness of John's tone forced Patrick to return the handbag with all its contents. Later, John personally went to the lady's house to return the handbag. She was absolutely delighted by this act and told John that she would have stopped coming to the store if they had not returned her bag as she was certain that she had left it there. Patrick also mentioned to the lady that their cashier helped in finding the handbag, so the credit goes to him as well. The management of the store appreciated the decisions made by John in this situation and the efforts of Patrick in finding the handbag as they ensured the retention of a loyal customer. John made sure that no one found out that Patrick was trying to steal the handbag. This way he was able to gain Patrick's trust, and taught him the importance of integrity and true leadership.

Through John's story it has become clear that integrity is the most important characteristic that a leader could have. The achievement of the aims and objectives of a business rely on the quality of the manager. It not only allows the leader to work more efficiently, but it also brings his/her followers onto the right path just like John guided Patrick to do the right thing. As you continue to read this book further you will find out about various other traits that are essential for an individual to possess to be a successful and effective leader.

"The glue that holds all relationships together, including the relationship between the leader and the led is trust, and trust is based on integrity."

Brian Tracy

Chapter 6
Tolerance

"The highest result of education is tolerance."

Helen Keller

Tolerance is one of those traits, which holds the secrets behind the success in life. Not only in business but in personal life and personal affairs, tolerance is that one quality which gives you the ability to be kind and compassionate toward everyone. As it is evident by what Helen Keller has said in the quotation mentioned above, a person who is well-educated and full of wisdom always shows tolerance toward the mistakes and wrongdoing of other people. This chapter is going to inform you about the importance of tolerating the acts of workers and giving them a chance to grow and learn from their mistakes.

Before we get into the specifics of how the characteristic of tolerance in a business owner affects an organization, let us first build up an understanding of what tolerance really is. Every person bears a unique mindset, having a wide range of thoughts, ideas and opinions residing within his or her minds. The ability of a person to understand and accept the different opinions of other people is known as tolerance. The term 'tolerance' is sometimes also associated with the level of resistance in a person for a certain thing. Now it can be other people's actions, their habits or opinions which you might find to be very different from that of your own, but how much you are able to tolerate those things is your capacity of tolerance.

Mistakes Are How We Learn

Being a business owner or a manager, it is important to realize all the staff members are indeed human beings and that they can sometimes make mistakes. Usually, in enterprises, specifically if we talk about small businesses, it is mostly observed that the employees are ridiculed or insulted by the managers regarding the mistakes that they make while fulfilling their tasks. Such an attitude, when borne by the workers, starts to make the employees dissatisfied with the working environment and automatically brings inefficiency in their performance. As a manager you need to have a certain level of tolerance for the employee's mistakes as making mistakes is a part of their learning and development process. It is quite unnatural for an employer to think that his subordinates are not going to make any mistakes. It is understandable that at the time of hiring an individual, through tests and interviews, it is confirmed if the person is right for the job or not. However, in the beginning, the working environment is still quite new for that employee therefore, he or she will take some time to understand how things are done in this company. In this period, the employee will make some mistakes thus, the employer needs to tolerate those mistakes and should give some time to the worker to settle into the environment.

Other than that, an employer needs to understand that mistakes are indeed a part of life, whether they are work related or about the affairs of normal life. Sometimes, a person might be facing some major issues in his or her life outside the office, which can sometimes affect the performance of that individual in the workplace. who knows it, he or she experienced a death of someone close to them or they have a medical condition due to which it became hard for them to work properly? There can be numerous reasons behind the discrepancies found in an employee's performance. So, before you lash out on the employee, you must tolerate the staff member's behavior to a certain extent and give him or her some time to improve their performance. In such circumstances, it is always better to provide constructive feedback to the employee. As previously stated, the manager needs to have an open form of communication that you can ask the employee about their performance.

The sustainability of the growth of an organization is directly proportional to learning and development of the people who are involved in all its operations. As I mentioned before, the employees will not learn to do the work in the best possible manner until and unless they make a few mistakes.

A workplace which promotes a tolerant environment makes the employees feel more comfortable in applying their new ideas, which may seem more beneficial to them in performing a certain task related to the business. To improve the operations and the processes of the company, innovation is very important. And a worker can never act upon his or her innovative ideas until he or she is sure that if this new idea turns into a failure, they will not be degraded on that basis. This is only possible when a manager has enough tolerance toward the mistakes of the employees. If they are only provided with a proper feedback on their failed attempts, it will become easier for the employees to identify the parts where they are wrong, due to which they will avoid making such mistakes in the future.

Encouraging Workplace Tolerance

The culture and environment of a workplace are two main things which can be considered as the foundation of the operations of a business. To run the business smoothly, it is very important to focus on the kind of culture that prevails in the company. A culture rich in tolerance has a significant impact on the overall production efficiency of the company. When the management and the people, who reach the upper levels of the hierarchy of the company, encourage tolerance by showing how tolerant they are through their actions, and through this they pass their quality down to the workers and employees.

If we consider the overall impact of tolerance on the organization, it is very essential for the staff members to be able to tolerate each other. All the employees come from different backgrounds and possess a wide range of knowledge in certain areas, which they like to apply in the tasks assigned to them. If the workers are working on individual assignments, there are not many differences observed among the employees. However, when it comes to group projects, where the employees must work in a team, then it is important for them to respect and tolerate the opinions of other teammates. Teams will fail to show quality in their work, and they will also not be able to meet the deadlines for the delivery of their work if the team members lack tolerance for one another. It is also the responsibility of the managers to make sure that the employees get along well with each other so that the overall working productivity increases.

"In order for teams to be at their best, in order for us to leverage the full potential of groups of human beings, their ability to collaborate is everything," says management specialist,

Karen Gately

An organization can never manage to flourish if it does not pay attention to the betterment and healthiness of its employees. If you want to make sure that all of your business processes take place in an effective manner, then it is essential for you to create a working environment for your subordinates which is not only comfortable for them, but also gives them a peace of mind. It is often seen that people become victims of several emotional disorders like anger, anxiety and worst of all, depression, after they are introduced to a professional working environment. These emotional instabilities not only make it difficult for them to give an outcome, proficient, but their personal lives are also affected by it. Many individuals experience these symptoms because they are subjected to constant ridiculing and degradation by their superiors. If their working efficiency has been affected, then they are either mocked or are scolded in front of their colleagues, which is not only shameful for them, but they also become the victims of constant workplace bullying.

Therefore, to avoid such harmful effects of the workplace, it is important for the managers to make sure that they tolerate the minor mistakes of the workers. Even if they feel the need of pointing out the issues in the performance of the employee, it is very important for them to discuss the matter privately and provide them with positive feedback with a sole purpose of guiding and assisting the staff member. Managers should understand the fact that they are the role models for the employees and a source of inspiration. If you, as a manager, show tolerance toward the employees, they will start feeling more comfortable in interacting with you, which would lead to achievement of higher efficiency in their work.

Knowing the Difference between Tolerance and Ignorance

It is important for you to understand the difference between tolerance and ignorance. Especially when it comes to the organizations, it is extremely crucial for a manager to know the extent of tolerance needed for certain behaviors or actions.

For instance, when an employee shows up late for work once or twice in a month, then that is something tolerable which a manager should let go and not reprimand him or her on such a thing. But, if the staff member makes it a habit and comes to the office late every other day, then the manager will be ignorant to not act against the employee. In an organization, discipline is important, otherwise the ways in which the operations of the business are run can be affected adversely.

When you manage a business, you need to draw a clear line between the things that are acceptable in your workplace and the intolerable activities. This line should not only be visible to the managers, but you need to make sure that the employees are also able to understand the difference between both as well. Among the many duties of a manager, creating a zero-tolerance policy can assist in providing guidance and a clear message for employee's workplace behavior.

One of the simplest examples of a zero-tolerance policy would be the deadline of delivery of work. Let's say a person works 9 hours a day, on a regular shift of 8am to 5pm, in which he or she has a one-hour lunch break. The employee needs to make sure that their work is completed by 5pm before they leave the office. Now, sometimes, it is understandable that the worker is not able to achieve his/her targets for the day due to certain reasons such as a lot of meetings or training sessions during that day. Under those circumstances, it is acceptable for the employer to understand that the employee had a valid reason behind the failure to complete the task during the day. But if the staff member makes it a habit to delay the work daily. Then the manager should devise a certain policy to avoid such behavior from the employees. Sometimes it is observed that the worker wastes a lot of time like taking extensive breaks or even exceeding their lunch breaks. There are numerous ways to avoid this loss of productive time. You, as an employer, can offer a certain incentive for the workers who manage to deliver quality work in the specified amount of time. This way people who take long breaks and exceed their lunch breaks will be losing out on more potential salary increases, and it is true that no one likes even a penny less than their specific amount of income when they receive the pay-check.

This way the employees will not only get to know about the actions, which are not tolerated by the company, but in fact they will also understand the kind of consequences they would be facing if they do a certain thing. To provide you a better understanding of how a manager needs to have tolerance, let's take a look at a scenario. Albert is a manager at a textile factory, which mainly produces garments like cotton pants and jeans. Now there is a huge number of staff members who work at the factory, and Albert is responsible for the performance of those workers.

There is an individual named Peter who is one of the subordinates of Albert, and he is mostly assigned a task to check the stitching of at least 200 pairs of pants and then send them for final ironing. One day, Peter was not able to send 200 pieces for final ironing and instead only sent 150 pieces. When Albert inquired about the lack of production, Peter informed him, he was not feeling well, so it was hard for him to work that day. Albert did not say anything and just lightly informed Peter to make sure that he completes his work before he leaves.

However, the same thing happened the next week, but Albert ignored considering that there must have been an issue faced by Peter. In the third week, it was observed that Peter made it a habit and started to take advantage, considering that the management did not take any strict actions when the employees delayed their work. What is even worse is that the other employees also adopted the same approach. As a result, in a matter of a few days, the entire supply chain was affected since the factory failed to deliver its large orders because of this prevailing habit among the staff. The efficiency and skills of Albert then became questionable. To deal with this matter, Albert quickly conducted a meeting with Peter and suspended him for a week for intentional delay in the completion of work. Furthermore, he came up with a policy at the factory that every worker had to meet their target for the day with the exception of three days' maximum in a month when the work was not delivered on time. If the worker delayed the work for more than three days in a month, the salary of the days in which he or she failed to meet the deadlines would be deducted by fifty percent. By taking such drastic measures, Albert is once again able to manage the performance of his employees or subordinates and managed to maintain proper production.

Considering the scenario that we just discussed, it has become clear that tolerance is indeed important to maintain a healthy working environment, but when tolerance turns into ignorance, then it can become very dangerous for the organization as well. It is indeed acceptable to let the employees make mistakes in order to give them an opportunity to learn from them, but if the worker turns such things into habits, then that is the point where the manager needs to take serious action.

Chapter 7
Mindset

"Leadership is a mindset in action. So, do not wait for the title. Leadership isn't something that anyone can give you - you have to earn it and claim it for yourself."

Travis Bradberry

Hope is society's paradigm of balancing the bitter realities of present and past. Trust your instincts. Trust is the first step towards building any type of strong relation or commitment, regarding life, work, personal relations, and conduct in life. Our mind works in amazing ways in shaping our conduct. So, trusting yourself, with the realization of your position is the first step towards success. Realization is the first battle you have won. If you realize where you stand in the whole scenario, you have already won half the battle because now you know your strengths and areas for improvement. Acknowledging the areas in which you are lacking allows you to focus your efforts and understanding there.

Preparation and upbringing of a healthy mindset is far more difficult than the preparation of the physical body. It is the mind that directs a person's specific characteristics into his/her qualities and abilities. As for a secret intelligence agent, if you think there is a breach to your cover, consider it already blown long ago, the fact that you are realizing it now is because you might have not trusted your instincts. Your mind is a central hub of an individual's body. It is the mindset that differs one person from another and a person from an animal, with the ability to think, react, feel, to counteract, manipulate among other things. Thus, having a positive state of mind with an optimistic vision to overcome any flaws will help you, your organization, and your business to flourish and reach new heights of success.

Having a healthy mind would not only be beneficial for yourself, but you might also be able to mold another person's pessimistic perspective into an optimistic one. Personality traits are like a person's manual with specific characteristics and qualities that impact their nature and persona. Our mind adapts. Our brain is in a constant state of learning and storing memories, data, information, and visual stimuli. Everything is being stored in either a pictorial form or in numbers and figures. Therefore, your brain is constantly working, evoking ideas, generating senses, suggesting commands on how to operate your body. All these functions help you decide your next move.

You can mold and change your brain to think and react in a specific way, in a way that suits your needs. Psychological aspects can affect your mindset significantly in numerous ways such as how your business or job would be able to succeed, and the effectiveness of the decisions you make on your work. How is your relationship toward your co-workers and subordinates? Because it is these people, who make you the 'leader' or the 'boss', which also implies that their behavior toward you are highly reflected by your conduct toward them. If you are the roof of a structure, your subordinates are the pillars that are holding the roof in its deserved position.

Being hopeful solves many problems from everyday life to the biggest emotional, physical, or social problems as well. Hope gives you strength. It enables you to counter your trouble and get back on to your feet, regaining the conscious state of mind and to make better decisions on how to deal with the problem with effective and positive outcomes. Even if temporarily, hope evokes a sense of self reassurance and strength, it gives you the courage to counter your problems rather than giving up. Hope is like a lamp in a dark isolated room, it is the first step toward believing. Believing in the existence of your current circumstances as well as future aspirations. When you have created a goal, you start working on it to either improve the current plan or continue with on the same path. It is up to you to decide on which side on the line you want to be. Expectation sets peoples' souls on fire; it is what makes people believe in a better tomorrow. Perceiving the fullness of time, hope provokes people to do well in life and improve their conduct in life toward others, believing they will get tenfold in return as written in the Bible. It makes people believe in the concept of love and reward, holding this world together in its exact shape. Hope is an escape from reality into the land of your vision. It is what makes you get out of your bed every day and take hold of your responsibilities. Hope is not believing that everything is perfect, but hope is what makes people believe in a time of crisis that it will stop hurting soon.

Life is never perfect; it is your ability to make every little thing in your surroundings, which excites you about your existence, worth it. Life is a series of ups and downs that help a person to gain some stability by going through several experiences, which are sometimes good and sometimes bad. Based on your experiences, the memories have an impact on your mindset. Therefore, make sure to avail every good aspect and memory from your daily life so that whenever you feel down, those memories will be there to maintain your positivity.

Before even stepping into the field of business or any other field, it is imperative for an individual to analyze himself/herself and characterize their instincts and qualities on the basis of their personality traits and how they can improve themselves. This would help that individual in identifying their weak points. By doing so, they would be able to guide and help others in the same areas. Personality is what embeds a person's perception into the mind of the audience. For we all know the book is always judged by its cover, no matter what. You get to know about a person's nature as time passes by. During the first meeting with an individual will judge their behavior and the actions. It is essential to improve your mindset first, resulting in an overall more positive personality. Point to note, is that people can read even the slightest of change in your behavior through your gestures and body movements.

However, the 'boss' manages his/her subordinates and commands the employees to get the specific task done under the boundaries of the deadline whereas, a 'leader' inspires them and boosts their will to get the work done. Anyone can be a boss, but not everyone can be a leader. It requires a specific set of skills, leadership qualities and positive personality traits. Every organization has a boss, it is essential to improve your mindset first, resulting in an overall more positive personality. needs are a leader to help flourish the sales and improve productivity of the team. Leaders do not manipulate their employees' opinions, but rather they consider the suggestions from them to help draw a valid conclusion for the betterment of the company. Leaders can also work effectively in different aspects of life such as in their personal conduct, their relationships, their everyday life chores, and socializing with people. Leaders are more often successful and have an amazing persuasive persona that attracts people and makes them show that they are worthy enough of their trust. Leaders tend to ensure that the employees do not feel insecure at work. They do not use negative reinforcement to get the work done, rather he/she motivates the employee to be more productive. Leaders offer equality in every aspect whether its job opportunity, equal wages, bonuses, incentives or valuing their opinions. Leaders invest in their employees in building their personality and helping them adopt some traits to be a better version of themselves, as the leaders focus on long term planning. Leaders listen to their employees, and they know the importance of seeking and incorporating their opinions in the process of decision making. Leaders motivate their employees by emphasizing the importance of time and efficiency.

What is going through a person's mind is reflected through his verbal and nonverbal expressions, movements, gestures and postures as well. This allows one to determine how their coworker is feeling, which helps that individual in reacting accordingly. A valuable leadership skill is the ability to understand another person's personality traits and use this knowledge when working with that individual. Helping your potential partners can help in stabilizing the financial condition of the organization as well as improve the relation among every employee from every level of the chain. This would help in developing trust, empathy and devotion towards their work, workplace, their colleagues, and their boss.

Mental illness is considered as a disability, and it rightfully should be. Diseases like anxiety or depression corrode a person's body from inside, leaving just a hollow structure. They eat you from the inside slowly and gradually they push the individual further into the zone of complete darkness and isolation. Mental illness puts a stop to a person's thinking and his/her ability to move and proceed further toward a brighter tomorrow.

Peer group plays a vital role in the upbringing and counseling of a person's brain. Peer groups are always present no matter what phase of life there are in. The phrase *"you're known by the company you make"* makes more sense by the time you grow and mature and realize some of the peer group members share a common mindset and ideology toward every object and have a mutual understanding of the situations they are in. They can either confine a person's thinking into a closed space or make them think beyond their average thinking capacity, helping them expand their previous mindset. Peer pressure or the term, 'social pressure' signifies one person influencing or pressuring another person's thoughts or actions. When we are in a peer group we tend to adopt the same principles, thoughts, or actions which are not necessarily considered peer pressure but instead simply a change because of our new environment, by observing the natural behavior from their 'peer group'.

Peer pressure can be direct and at most times, indirect as well which can be perceived through the behavioral attitude or performance of your group. As an example, think about a classroom, the highest achiever always has an impact on the mindset of others. Either their mind accepts it as a challenge or a threat depending on the qualities and the positivity of the student towards the subject. The achievement of one student sets a precedent, which most of the students are compelled to achieve and thus creates a healthy atmosphere of learning. Furthermore, how a mind can affect the productivity of an individual's efficiency is determined by how he adapts to the changes from his/her surroundings and how he/she responds is adaptation. In a person's surrounding they can be exposed to cultural, sexual, and religious diversities which can help an individual have a well-rounded mindset. Exposure to different types of experiences can be gained from traveling. Traveling helps a mind grow and introduces it to the set of new emotions from the surroundings. Exposure to new techniques broadens the horizons of a person's vision and thought process, which helps them work on a relatively bigger scale, resulting in positive outcomes.

Mindset is one of the biggest examples of how our brain is tricked into admitting the presumably facts and ordering our body on how to perform placebo. The brain sends signals to the different parts of the body convincing our consciousness into thinking that the pill that we just took is going to be a relief from the pain we are experiencing.

Whereas all it does is just satisfy our demand of consuming medicine and that makes it effective. The medicine may have not treated the pain, but rather our brain is successful in convincing ourselves that the pain has been cured. One of the experiments related to how mindset works and how it can direct a person's thinking towards certain emotions and reactions was carried out by one of the famous

Professor, Mr. Fabrizio Benedetti. He conducted an experiment regarding the effectiveness of placebo in the treatment of Parkinson's disease. Benedetti came across the effect of placebos while researching pain management. The results contributed more to his amusement when he found out that patients who were given a dose of placebos faced a decrease in the rate of rising neurons by up to 40%, which enabled the patients to move and function with more ease.

Having a healthy mindset in a business is as important in any field of study. This is because we do not take mental health issues as seriously as we should. Not all minds need medical attention, but we do need to pay attention to how we are feeling and have healthy ways to cope. We are focusing on our physical well-being every day, which, I admit, holds immense importance as well. We are constantly in the state of denial that our mental health is the key to shaping our physical fitness. This point cannot be stressed enough as mental health is no doubt a serious aspect, which cannot be ignored. You might come across a lot of people who go to gym every day for physical fitness, but you might have not come across any single person that meditates, or does some specific mind exercises in order to improve the mental state of their mind. Ups and downs are a part of life and an important aspect of any business. Every business must go through a series of different phases at every stage to grow. As a leader you have the highest responsibility compared to your subordinates, the higher the rank, the greater the responsibility. If a company fails in its project, the blame falls on the leader, and it is up to the leader how he tackles that issue and rises back on his/her feet.

The mindset of a leader is reflected through the productivity and satisfaction of the employees as well as from the progress of the company. If the employees are happy, they will take their work as a challenge rather than a burden. Moreover, the leader can ensure employees' satisfaction by providing them with a friendly work environment, where the employees' suggestions are heard.

If a leader is at ease and his mind is at peace, he will make sure that his subordinates, too, are at ease. This could be achieved through the leader's conduct toward his employees. The positive mindset of a leader ensures the success of any company's progress and prosperity. A healthy, positive, and progressive mindset leads to not just an increase in the efficiency and productivity of the employees, but also enables the organization to be successful.

"Real leaders do not cover up concerns; they guide and assist individuals with PTSD and Suicidal ideation".

Chapter 8
Consistency

"Consistency is one of the biggest factors in leading to accomplishment and success."

Byron Pulsifer

Consistency yields excellence, but it requires a lot of effort to be consistent as it is the most inconsistent thing in the whole world. It is one of the most important building blocks of any successful business empire. At any stage of a business, being consistent provides results either in the form of greater employee efficiency or managing relations with your clients and most importantly, in consumer satisfaction.

For instance, if you own a restaurant, you need to not only be productive, have productive ideas for incorporating new trends into your marketing, but consistency in good quality. Quality is what initially attracts customers while consistency will ensure that they continue to come back. Moreover, if a leader is inconsistent in any business, it can disrupt the whole chain of descending commands, from the manager to the employees to the supplier and eventually, the consumer.

"Without consistency there is no moral strength."
John Owen

The Key to Success in Long Term Planning

Consistency is a long-term plan that yields excellence and higher profits. Do not lose hope if you do not initially achieve the results you expected or if your planning changes throughout; every qualitative output requires time.

With consistent devotion and commitment to your work goal, you can achieve the high levels of success not needed or that you originally planned. It might take some time to reach it but that does not mean you have lost the race; everyone will achieve their goals in their own time. The core aspect of financial discipline is the long-term financial plans, which require a lot of commitment and consistency.

What many people tend to do when they do not achieve their expectations, is continually switching from one profession or path to another which changes their priorities as well as breaches their goal of long-term planning. You might have come across a lot of people in the field who left their passions either because the results did not turn out to be as what they expected or they couldn't bear staying consistent in the field. The worst part of this is some people even lose their dream and sight of financial plans and start to act all enigmatic and irresponsible without realizing that they are in fact pushing themselves into a bigger loss. This loss can be a loss of investment or debt which can be difficult to overcome.

"Long term consistency trumps short term intensity"
Bruce Lee

It is not about being perfect, it is about not giving up, no matter what the circumstances are. It is about staying firm in your ideas, the goals you have planned for yourself and for the future of your enterprise. As a leader, your responsibility is even greater since you need to ensure that all of your employees are engaged and invested in the long-term goal. For that you need to build up the consistency within the firm as well as your personality, your mood, your temper, your decision making, your perspective, your deliverance and everything that creates an impact on the person in your surroundings.

As soon as you adopt this trait, then the company will see more success. It will help your nuanced skills as a leader to be polished as well as prove to be beneficial in terms of your business growth and expansion over a longer period. It will also help in minimizing the risks of possible future losses by predicting the current position of your business, such as current monthly gains and potential downfalls, and what could be the possible consequences if urgent measures are not taken.

Going to the gym in January with the high spirits of New Year resolution might be easy but staying on the treadmill even on the hottest day of June is difficult. Hence, consistency is not an easy process that can be achieved in an estimated span of time, but it is not impossible either.

Everybody wants consistency whether it is regarding daily life or professional life. Whether it is conducting business, investing, supervising employees, or dieting, everything requires consistency and time to yield fruitful results. It develops your routine and builds momentum; your routine becomes habitual to the point that it is infused into your personal nature.

For example, if we take a sample from our daily life, it requires a lot of dedication, patience, efforts, hard work and a great amount of exercise to lose weight to become healthy and fit. This process does not take effect overnight. But at the end, you will be content to see the outcome of your long-term dedication, and an award for your hard work and dedication to the goal.

"Success is neither magical or mysterious. Success is the natural consequence of consistently applying basic fundamentals."

Jim Rohn

Stability and Growth

Being consistent is one of the major differences that distinguishes success and failure. It ensures stability and growth; it lays the foundation for any successful business operation. Being persistent will help you obtain your goals, but to maintain your goal you need consistency.

Moreover, anything that is codependent or is more than a one man's job has lesser probability of consistency as you can control or manage everyone and everything at the same time. That's why every person involved in a chain of process needs to give in their 100% in order to achieve the desired results. Keeping all the employees consistent at their job is the responsibility of the leader.

Trial and Error

Consistency saves you from facing any major losses before diving into the sea of unknown. Knowing the behavioral pattern of something helps you predict the next action that is going to be taken, and helps you prepare yourself either to endure it or to counter it in the most efficient way possible. To launch a new product or introduce a new marketing technique, a company needs to go through all the previous track records of the sales and losses, if any. Additionally, track records for the gross revenue and profits are also considered before creating a new plan.

As far as judgment is concerned, you cannot decide whether that thing is right or wrong until you have used it or observed it for a longer period. This rule applies to almost every aspect of life whether personal or professional. overtime, one can see different trends and can make a more accurate prediction on the next move.

This aspect helps the company to not face any big losses or jolts due to unsuccessful implementation, but it also provides room for measurements to be taken to counteract those mishaps. Every person learning from their mistakes and consistency helps us overcome our flaws.

As for a leader's perspective, typically implying new initiatives, process, and organizational structures at least six months before judging them either a success or a failure could be greatly beneficial. If the system is in favor of the pros with just minor tweaking instead of the major overhauls, then it is worth a shot.

Leaders Can Make Product a Brand – Roadmap to success

Consistency establishes an overall reputation and certain standards that people expect from you every time they come to you for your product or service. No matter what the consequences are, people always expect the same once their expectations have developed. As a consumer, the last thing you would want is to be disappointed. As a leader, you must understand the basic human instinct that your employees and customers expect consistency. This proves that people want predictability. The bitter reality is that we all live in an unpredictable world where people get happy when they get what they expect and they return to avail the same quality in terms of taste, service, or anything that your product promises and showcases.

Consistency lies in the core of any successful brand no matter what the circumstances are, the consumers expect the people behind the brand to deliver them the same experience whether speaking of a product or a service. A Kit-Kat chocolate bought in Canada should taste the same as the one bought in Turkey or anywhere else in the world. Great brands deliver consistent quality regardless of the location, as the main goal is to satisfy the expected needs of the consumers.

A track record of success is required for any business to grow into a brand. You cannot have a track record if you keep jumping from one platform to another or trying new tactics. Many efforts and plans, which are supposed to yield greater productive outcomes, fail even in the beginning before reaching the finishing line. This usually happens not because the tactics or the plan devised had any loopholes, but because the team simply did not stay determined to achieve the desired objective.

Making Sure Everyone is on the Same Page – Actions Speak Louder than Words

Consistency can foster a unified group of subordinates in your team. It is not confined to the quality of the products or services only; the change comes always from within. For a company to deliver consistent quality, they are supposed to establish consistent measures within the creative field first, which is reflected through your product. A firm must deliver consistent values on every job, equal opportunities, and an unbiased workplace.

This would help the firm build a smooth bond between the leader and the employee, therefore resulting in smoother production and efficient team works. Although some factors might make ensuring consistency a challenge, such as many teams working parallel in the same firm. To overcome such hurdles, a leader should devise a process that is systematic in its reliance on investigation, observation, exploration, feedback, and refinement.

A leader must be a walking example for his/her subordinates. Your employee acts more to how you act rather than what you ask. One of the most effective leadership qualities is establishing trust in the workplace. Nobody is going to follow your commands if they do not have faith in you, and to accomplish big goals, you need a team. Trust requires constant maintenance to grow over the period. And if a leader has already mastered the art of incorporating trustworthiness amongst the subordinates; the next big step is being successful. Employees, who share a mutual bond of trust with their leaders, are proven to be more engaged, concerned, motivated, and willing to fix the problems within the organization.

As for a leader, you must be consistent throughout, build a relationship of trust or to shape the conduct of the employees. Employees often adapt to leadership behaviors and attitudes, which they observe rather than the motivational speeches given behind closed doors. For instance, if you promise to show up somewhere or meet someone, ensure that you follow through. If you are showing up late for a meeting, then do not expect your subordinate behaving the same way as you did.

If you have the same expectations from every individual of the team, make sure you are enforcing the rules and implying ideas the same way to everyone. Even in the worst of times, your team will know they can rely on you to be reliable and fair by being consistent in your behavior, actions, and expectations.

Consistency- A Critical Leadership Trait

Proceeding further, some employees might not mind the constant changes, but most of them prefer consistency. Creating a plan and constantly deviating from that by changing policies and the procedures can be taxing. Work environment seems more organized, under control, and less chaotic if the operations, practices, and procedures are consistent.

By creating the atmosphere of consistency among the workplace, you can make your employees more efficient with their productivity level. It also helps to ensure that your customer and employees feel comfortable and familiar within the workplace. If given the choice for a boss, which would you choose? A boss that is a jerk but is predictable or a boss that balances between being fair and unfair daily?

Subordinates often prefer a supervisor with a predictable cocky attitude rather than the one with dynamic mood swings, who constantly dwells between fairness and unfairness. A mercurial behavior from the supervisor has proven to induce higher physiological stress levels among the employees than those who are constantly being treated the same way by their 'jerk' boss. For instance, a high-producing salesperson who often gets leaves without pay deduction or is unnoticed on coming late; such cases increase the risk of conflict amongst the fellow colleagues rather than building a competition. Instead of working together to get up, employees start working to bring others down. If the leader opts for favoritism instead of being fair, loyal, and engaged to the firm, the workplace becomes almost impossible to work in.

When you are consistent with your words and actions you build an atmosphere of trust. People know where they stand in that situation and how they are supposed to react. They have faith in you and your reflexes, and they are not hesitant or reluctant towards sharing their ideas and even admitting the wrong or mistakes they made.

One of the most important leadership qualities is to be consistent in your personality since inconsistency in moods, behaviors, dealing with the problem, treating employees and such breed fear and uncertainty throughout the workplace. This, as a result, makes employees believe that every day will be a new surprise.

Consistency in Mood

Great leadership requires emotional health, which includes controlling emotions. Although there is no exact way to manage your emotions on an hourly basis, the job gets much more difficult under critical circumstances. But let us be real, there is nothing more disruptive than a person with constant mood swings in the workplace, especially if that person is in a leading position.

A leader's mood is always reflected on the productivity of the subordinates and their productivity. Be particular about managing emotions if you had a rotten morning or if the organization is undergoing critical circumstances. We all have days where we feel like everything is going wrong when incidents such as whether it is spilling our coffee, forgetting our wallet, or leaving the keys in the car. Being in the leading position, bringing change is the key to success, do not cater to emotions that accompany the change process. Your bad mood can negatively affect others.

Manage emotions before they manage you. For some people listening to music before showing up at the workplace helps divert their attention from a certain problem they are facing, while for some it could be reading the faith-driven leadership lessons. All individuals need to be aware how their actions can have a positive influence on someone else. For a leader, a problem should never be a distraction, but rather he/she should accept it as a challenge and strategic enabler for the continuous improvement and opportunities that were previously unseen.

Optimism, enthusiasm, and respect are contagious; when you show up to work happy and with a positive, serious, and productive mood, you lead the establishment of a strong foundation. Leaders in specific, not bosses, know how to set the mood and how to be emotionally and mentally stable, competent, healthy and humble so that others can do their jobs with equal enthusiasm. If you are at the brink of a mood swing, remind yourself that your every move is being watched and learned from, as well as you are setting a pathway for others to act upon. In other words, being a leader makes you a role model.

Consistency in Problem Solving

As a leader, you must adopt the strategy of two-way dialogue communication, rather than monotonous monologue. Always remember to communicate properly and authentically to create a more open environment, which encourages others to share their views and opinions as well. Do not be unpredictable. Be consistent with your nature, so that employees will know your stance on the situation and how they are supposed to be reacting to this.

As a leader you must establish a culture in a workplace that promotes learning, improvisation, empowerment, and innovation. Do not assume everyone knows what you are thinking. If you have invested enough time in building your team, you will know the mental capability of every person. Remove the sand between the gears through effective communication and direction. To stay calm under pressure, it is important to get a hold of your consciousness and stabilize your emotions under stressful situations. If your employees must walk on eggshells, it is high time for you to realize and reevaluate your conduct toward them. Your workers should have a firm belief in you and your problem-solving skills through your consistent predictable positive behavior.

Consistency in passion for work

Consistency is more important than engaging in any work field. In establishing a business, one must consistently deliver value and quality to the consumers. If you can manage a consistent service and quality, you can work on promoting positive and consistent image.

Employees look up to their bosses to adopt certain qualities, which they are expected to deliver. When they work together, they have faith in you that without a doubt you, as a leader, will be standing by their side no matter what. Your work should demonstrate your passionate commitment so that others can follow your footsteps.

Passion is a zeal, an emotion, an urge that comes from within. You do not want to just perform your daily task without taking any interest in that. You should and must put all your passion into achieving the goal and upgrading your position.

As a leader, you must be consistent with everything you convey both verbally or nonverbally through your words and gestures. People working for you always look up to you as an example to behave and shape their conduct in the field. Be a beacon of wisdom and guidance for them in every aspect by being consistent throughout the process. Whatever leadership traits and managing techniques you imply, implement them consistently, do not lose hope. Consistent traits work as an anchor in stabilizing a company's performance and help in prolonging its excellence. Although it is crucial to say but inconsistency and leadership are two juxtaposed ideas, either a leader would be consistent, or he or she will not be a leader.

Chapter 9
Development

"The Growth and Development of people is the highest calling of Leadership."
Harvey S. Firestone

Development– The continuous process of improvising within the defined limits is known as development. It is referred to as the progress of striving for the best and not settling for the rest. Development is one of the core elements of building any successful leadership. It helps individuals to improve by learning from their past mistakes and external factors. To become a good leader, you need to have keen observation quality as well as above-the-chart personality traits to judge and guide your subordinates. Since an organization or a business is established through the efforts and contribution of every building block, strengthening the pillars holding the structure together is immensely important. Subordinates are the pillars that hold the organization in its shape and are pretty much responsible for the outcomes of any operation.

Fostering a unified group of subordinates is the first and foremost responsibility of a leader. The person in charge should know how to merge and yield better productive results from the team – by unifying them on a single cause. A good leadership trait always lays emphasis on unity and ideology amongst the team members. Successful leadership calls for leading a team of potential individuals with a mutual vision and motivation level rather than handling a disjointed chain of command.

To get all the subordinates on the same page is the job of the leader. He or she should be able to bring together all the members and their ideas by providing them with a platform to share their views and opinions. Reaching to a conclusion by mutually sharing opinions helps teams unite and strengthens their bond, since everyone develops a sense of being heard they tend to be outspoken and innovative.

Development within or outside the organization helps promote growth. Development is more than bound to just infrastructural modification and building of material. Development can be achieved through and within any medium or object. Business development entails a series of tasks and processes being carried out to achieve a unified goal. It can be about just improving the job program, or training the employees, or devising new strategies to help boost efficiency. The high performing companies are experts at recruiting, motivating, and most importantly developing their people.

Systematic use of technical operations and scientific knowledge to meet specific requirements to achieve a preset goal is referred to as development. Development, in business terms, is a long-term plan to create value for an organization from customers, market, employees, and market relationships. Regardless of how many techniques you adopt and how many sessions you conduct to spread awareness amongst your team members, the best type of development comes from within.

Actions speak louder than words. Your employees are more likely to adopt certain qualities by observing your conduct and approach toward it. As a leader you are always bound to meet certain expectations through your conduct in the field, your employees will always be observing your every move. Therefore, to maintain a decorum and create a professional yet learning atmosphere amongst the organization, a leader must exhibit certain qualities and actions which people want to see in him. As previously discussed, subordinates look to their leader as a gauge on decorum. To lead by example, a leader must engage in self-evaluation. Understanding the qualities, you need to improve, can benefit not only yourself but your employees as well. To lead by an example, you need to fix yourself first. Evaluate the areas where you lack in.

What are the areas you can strengthen? What are the certain qualities which you can adopt? Is the way you communicate viable enough for your employees to understand the command completely? What are the certain requirements that you expect from your employees? All this confusion and conflicts fall into the category of good business coaching.

How to build and develop your leadership skills?

To lead better, you need to learn better. Executive coaching plays a vital role in shaping the career as well as the personal conduct of a leader. Business coaching if done right, can do wonders – it can transform you from an average boss to a successful influential leader. This is a step towards development from within which eventually generates higher yield in the form of productivity from your team and even employees – act before you preach. Since a person who is leading needs to be up to date of all new trends as well as have a better understanding of the subject he or she is dealing in, executive coaching proves highly beneficial in directing their energy and efforts.

"I absolutely believe that people, unless coached, never reach their maximum potential."

Bob Nardelli

Learning about business leadership holds a meaningful prospect. Executive coaching helps leaders tackle their fears. Some businessmen are reluctant to step into new dimensions, as they fear the possible losses and setbacks. Business coaching helps businessmen reduce their self-doubting delusion by overcoming their dilemmas of falling into the pitfalls.

They provide businessmen with adequate resources and authentic strategies according to their needs and goals within their framework. Moreover, some leaders are constantly affected by their thoughts, which inevitably affects their work. Business coaching teaches the leaders how to prioritize their work with respect to time management techniques, without having to make them put any of their tasks in jeopardy. It is important for a leader to learn about the specific tricks and tips to tackle the hurdles of any situation they might come across. A leader's conduct and approach toward any situation are what sketch the traces for his employees to follow. Learning through the process of self-actualization and expertise helps leaders develop a perspective on. Once the leader gains perspective, it clears out the confusion and clarifies issues pertaining to any complex queries. Business coaching helps leaders build a vivid vision of the ground they are operating in. This results in increased productivity as well as creativity from the team.

A leader should be able to execute the plans and strategies without deviating from the context of the scenario. Simultaneously, a leader should be able to include all the factors that could somehow affect the outcome of the development process. Development is a crucial process, which requires training as well as awareness about every possible factor affecting your results. Therefore, business coaching helps you look at those unattended important areas, which some leaders fail to acknowledge. This learning process helps them in becoming a better version of themselves to become successful leaders.

Development and success go hand in hand. And to be a successful leader, you need to execute and achieve both. Although it might sound a bit ironic, a good leader is a person who leads and considers other's opinions. A leader is flexible in his personality toward his subordinates. A good leader is always open to new experiences and has room for improvements. Below are some traits which make a good leader; judge yourself on how well you are fulfilling these traits in your own life.

Inspire others

To attain the title of a successful leader, you need to determine your strategy of completing tasks. Your subordinates look up to you for inspiration. An effective leader should be able to motivate others and drive them to perform their best even in the worst-case scenarios – stability of a conscious mind. To become a great leader, you need to train yourself to become a better version of yourself every day. An effective leader brings growth and expansion, not within just himself but also in his subordinates, in the form of openness to creativity and new ideas. Inspire people working with and for you through your code of conduct;

consistency, motivation, dedication, and how you deal with the strenuous situations.

Do not close the doors for knowledge

You are never too old to gain knowledge. It is a myth that some people are born leaders. You always learn and adapt to changes you see. Some people might say that leadership qualities run in their genes – well that is because they are brought up in such an environment, which promotes leadership qualities. To some extent, I might agree with this personal intuition of being born with leadership skills, but to me, it is more of a talent than an earned position. We make mistakes and we learn from them, we learn and grow every day. It's like a never-ending loop – we follow before we lead.

Idolizing someone whom you look up to as your mentor while dealing with situations is also a form or learning. This chain continues once the people who used to be followers, become leaders themselves and start gaining followers who look up to them as well. Attaining knowledge is the most important building block of any development process. Without proper knowledge on the subject, you will not be able to process and execute properly. With everyday advancements in technology, it is difficult to stay up to date. But when the situation calls for some new development and approach, one should always look forward to seeking education regardless of the position or rank.

Communicate effectively – Be as clear as possible

Communication builds bridges between two related bodies and enables them to share their views to help understand each other better. Communication is one of the most powerful tools for any successful leader. A good communicator can solve a lot of problems just through his persuasive communication skills. A leader is supposed to not only be persuasive but also clear about their ideas and what he wants from the employees. Sometimes if the commands are not delivered properly, subordinates misinterpret the information which affects the quality of the work done.

A good communicator is not simply good at speaking or delivering, but the most important trait for a good communicator is to be a good listener. Through positive interaction, a good leader should be able to judge his employees through their communication power. Leaders provide a platform by unifying their subordinates to communicate and share their opinions. This, ultimately, generates a conclusion through two-way feedback.

Thinking out of the box – The bigger picture

A good leader is the one with a vision – a goal. You can pretty much imagine how it would be like for the subordinates to comply according to the demands if the person-in-charge has no clear picture of what is going on. Within the workplace, a good leader should be able to make predictive possible outcomes considering the failures and chances of success.

As a leader, you should never confine your thinking and your perspective at any point. You always need to think big and plan bigger. This is what makes you overcome your unpredicted challenges easily as well as it eliminates the fear of possible losses. As a part of an effective leadership, a good leader must be well-prepared for any immediate changes that may come his way, and that he ought to be able to perform his best regardless of the circumstances. A good leader should and must always foresee any possible trouble ahead of their schedule and tackle it by managing the least possible losses. Thinking out of the box helps a leader to become more open towards different ideas as well as it allows him/her to create a room for creativity. As one aspect is linked with another, a good leadership trait calls for the leader to be ahead of his time. A leader should and must make decisions based on exposure to different sexual, religious, and cultural diversification.

Act before you preach

Lead by an example as a model. To become a successful leader, you need to develop this personality trait in you. As a matter of fact, your subordinates look up to you whenever they feel the need to follow in the footsteps of a mentor. Since you are the closest and most easily approachable person to them, you will be observed through your actions, emotions, gestures, behavior, conduct, and reactions.

For instance, if you call for a meeting at 12 o'clock, arrive early and begin the meeting by 12 o'clock sharp. Don't cancel on meeting frequently unless there's an emergency, only then you may postpone or shift the time. How can you expect an employee to be on time if you, as a leader, are setting a bad example, by arriving late to scheduled events and meetings? How you react and perform in difficult situations exhibits your code of conduct, which is viewed and adopted by your employees. To maintain a healthy relationship and create a strong bond with your team members, you need to start working on your development and growth so that you can lead by example for them.

Moving ahead, the roof of any successful organization is suspended by the pillars, in this case, the pillars are the subordinates. The more you strengthen the pillars, the stronger and long-lasting your structure will be. The best type of investment an organization would ever make is the investment in its employees.

"The only thing worse than training your employees and having them leave is not training them and having them stay."
Henry Ford

As a leader, you expect your subordinates to be equal in all aspects; one is who can share the same ideology and match the level of your thinking. Basically, every manager loves to have highly skilled specialists on his team. To invest in a subordinate is to invest in building their leadership qualities; development, skills, growth and discovering their potential. As a leader, you want to see a part of yourself in every subordinate and continually maintain high expectations of them. Most leaders take employee management as a matter of option rather than essential need, which is a big mistake.

A company's most important asset is its employees. If you believe that hiring a person who is trained by another organization for a specific set of tasks rather than training him on your own, then that is a mistake you should not make. This employee will never be loyal to the organization as well as to their work. As a leader, it is your responsibility to shape your subordinates into becoming a successful leader, if it is their desire.

To feel devoted, employees expect some attention from the organization and that devotion is derived from how much the company is willing to invest in its employees. As a leader, you need to be aware of all such attributes required. As a successful leader, you may want to pass on your wisdom onto your subordinates to help them perform better and up to the mark. To meet your expectations, you need to guide them theoretically as well as practically regarding the ideas and strategies to excel in their respective fields. As a proficient leader, you must be capable of helping your subordinates in realizing as well as evaluating their full potential. For instance, through practical experiments, you can evaluate your employee's potential and his area of expertise, and certain other factors such as, the type of environment in which he is the most productive, or the amount of adequate lighting for him to work efficiently and so on.

One of the greatest qualities of successful leaders is that they are open regarding their experiences and past mistakes. They also emphasize on the lessons which those incidents have taught them. Therefore, it helps a leader in forming his employees the way he wants them to be by polishing their already existing skills and to direct their time and energy into the correct direction.

The four vital steps of developing your subordinates are:

Helping them discover their strengths

Since every employee is different, you cannot expect all of them to respond to the command in a unified manner. This is the most crucial step that lays the ground for future developments. Every employee has his own set of beliefs, preferences, cultural background, personal experiences, and values. Therefore, a good leader should be able to identify those distinctive qualities and features as well as he/she should know how to put them to use.

This could be a crucial step as it requires a leader to connect with their employees at an emotional level so that they may feel comfortable in stepping out of their comfort zone and stepping into a completely new environment. Once an employee has adjusted, they will be able to discuss and share ideas and information through which the leader can assess them.

As a leader, you need to be able to determine when to be outspoken and when to be silent. This skill can result in receiving great input and ideas from your employees. Do not throw a list of confusing rhetorical questions, instead make them feel good and comfortable in your presence and then assess and come to a judgment based on the situation being discussed. Just be direct, be real.

Recognizing their progress

Recognition and reward, the two most important R(s) of a successful development. Employees' recognition is the acknowledgment of the work, energy, effort, and improvement they have offered as a contribution to the development of the organization's success. Recognizing as well as rewarding employees for their efforts is immensely important to keep them motivated.

This critical step in development yields many positive outcomes. For instance, encouragement engages the employee and devotes their attention toward work. A reward in the form of a verbal compliment or just even a pat on the back could be sufficient in an employee's eyes, which would make them perform better. Moreover, it increases loyalty and retains the best talent as when employees feel appreciated, they tend to pay more attention to their work.

Appreciating employees for their work establishes a healthy supportive work environment that promotes healthy competition amongst the fellow employees. It also gives them a feeling of belonging within the organization, which improves their productivity.

Nurturing their skills

The best leader always pays attention toward developing his subordinates into leaders. Through nurturing the talent and skills of employees, a leader shows how much they value their employees, which is highly effective in yielding positive results and greater productivity level. An influential leader identifies the divine set of distinctive skills that each individual employee possesses, and so he encourages them to act in ways that are easy for them by creating an environment of learning and sharing. Development takes place when people are encouraged for their efforts and when they are provided with feedback on a regular basis.

A good leader can set goals for his employees, keeping into account all the factors associated with his/her area of interest and expertise. As an effective leader, one of the best things you can offer to your employee in this learning process of development is, enabling them to develop their decision-making ability. Sound decision making is imperative for an employee to achieve his/her goal and make the most out of any lingering opportunity.

Great leaders judge their employee's capabilities. A leader knows how his employee takes on a situation, and how they perform under pressure.

Managing their performance

Performance management refers to determining the performance and changes in an employee's conduct toward achieving the organizational goal. It is basically the ongoing assessment of your past and current experiences based on the performance, accountability, and outcomes. It consists of providing an employee with regular feedback, which is valuable in assisting him to pursue his future pre-set goals.

Define goals – be specific and smart. You must take into account the scientific as well as technological information while developing your goals. Align the goals along with the corporate strategy.

Offer feedback – a regular two-way feedback holds immense importance in any developing stage. While it motivates an employee, it also helps a leader to justify based on performance if the employee requires any assistance or coaching through programs, especially if the employee is working on a critical client. Although creating daily performance reports could be difficult for the managers however, it would be viable if done in a short period of time. Bonuses – one of the most important factors that keep us hooked to our daily jobs is the pay we receive at the end of the month. The pay-for-performance strategy can be used to retain the top talent of the organization.

This step, as already discussed, creates a sense of loyalty toward the organization. Through appraisal programs, you can keep a check and balance, and provide feedback regarding the performance, improvement and the steps that need to be taken. Such programs and strategies help develop a sense of healthy competition and promote employees to perform better to achieve as many incentives as possible. It keeps your top performers motivated while evoking a sense of continuous effort for the underperformers. Performance management is an efficient way of utilizing your company's time and money. It is also the key to create and manage an aligned up-to-date workforce.

Every individual has a great potential within themselves. It is the leader's job to work out those specific hidden talents and skills and use them for the organization's wellbeing.

Chapter 10
The People

"Leadership is unlocking people's potential to become better."

Bill Bradley

The crux of the whole business leadership system revolves around catering to people's needs and managing those needs to get maximum return out of it. People are the sole notion behind the technicalities of any business. And not to forget the fact, people, or your audience, are the most unpredictable, inconsistent part of the whole chain with their tentative tastes changing every day.

People, on either end of the business are important in carrying out a successful business outcome. Whether, in the form of transactions, finances, personal relationships, forming an alliance or any such business operations, people are the pillars holding the business in position. Your audience can directly alter your product's value. It all depends on the circumstances and changes in taste. With this everyday evolving scenario, more businesses are rushing toward adapting to the new changes to be better than others. And thus, to carry out a successful business plan, a leader must attain certain qualities to improvise its leadership skills to keep up with the pace and meet people's needs.

Let us talk about people. 100% of your customers are people and the same percentage accounts for all the employees working under you. So, if you fail to understand people, then it means you fail to understand business. The human factor sits at the core of any successful business leadership. The key factor of any organization's success is its trained people. The best organizations have the best people working for them at almost every level. It all starts from inception, which is the hiring process.

Every operation, outcome, and process of your company boils down to people. A business is a series of structural alliances of people, holding hands together like a chain, taking orders and passing them on till the last person on the other end receives the desired product or service. You will be able to lead more effectively by putting your theoretical strategies to practical implementation. By understanding the human factor, you can create brand loyalty amongst your consumers and keep them hooked to your product and services. Other than that, you will be able to close bigger and better deals by working effectively in a predictable environment with lesser chances of unexpected major losses. Considering this approach, it also forces you to consider your own motivations and strengths. Thus, this can eventually make you more empathetic and understanding.

Excellence in understanding people is the first step toward developing a high-performance culture within an organization. Nothing overcompensates the given responsibility and getting entrusted with a task, as employees feel more connected and familiar to the workplace when they are recognized.

Leadership and people go hand in hand – they cannot be separated. As a leader, you must be conscious of your qualities and traits since you are always being watched and adapted – the way you behave and react to certain situations. Your personal behavior and attitude toward people are two of the biggest chunks of your make-up and performance credibility as a leader. A negative attitude toward people and pessimistic approach toward work can be the biggest obstacle between you and your company's success. However, we are not denying the fact that most of the people are constantly battling through these trials to master these specific viable leadership traits. To maximize your returns and enjoy all these benefits, you need to embed the human element into your company's core values. Some of the steps to help you get started to work upon and improve your position are mentioned below.

As a Leader

- You must be envisioned of what lies beyond. Since you are in charge, set a destination and a clear objective for the whole organization to achieve.

- Be vocal and informative about what you want from your team? Create boundaries within which your team should operate.

- Provide clear instructions. What is involved in the assigned project? What is the budget? What is the deadline? Any area for leniency specifications regarding the client or the project is very essential to reach closer to the desired outcome.

- Involve your team and take input from them. Ask them for their suggestions and consider their opinions in drawing a mutual conclusion.

- Understand that it is not just about you, it is about the whole organization. Prioritize professional interests over your own.

- Motivate your team and identify their hidden potentials.

- Entrust your employees with tasks and make them feel they are being recognized by the organization.

- Pay keen attention toward the client's details and what the client wants – People on the other end of the business (consumers) are always right.

- Be intentional and let your subordinates know that you want them empowered as co-creators and that you value their efforts.

You Do Not Build Business, You Build People, Who, Then Build Your Business

What is the one thing you should do to grow your business faster? Grow your people. The development of people is reflected upon the growth of a business. How fast a business grows and expands, is dependent on the distinctive leadership qualities. Money is not the basic requirement of growth, although it can help to some extent. As a leader, you are entitled to bring your team on the same page and envision them with what you perceive to clear the thick cloud of confusion as they embark on the venture of growth.

Undoubtedly, in almost every process and operational systems, people play a vital role. The possessed knowledge acquired skills and attitudes often determine the quantity and quality of system output. The amount of efforts invested is reflected upon the type of output obtained. The efficiency of every individual is determined from the productivity level they achieve.

As a leader, you need to determine the distinctive qualities and strengths of your team. You should be able to identify their potentials and assign work accordingly to yield the best outcomes. For instance, just as an automobile needs right parts in the right places fitted and assembled by the right people, high-performance business systems require the right people for the required job to get the best positive outcomes. However, this is not as easy as it may sound, since most of the time a lot of business leaders fail to recognize the hidden potentials and eventually fail to empower their people. But not only is the identification of potential imperative, there are a lot of various factors that account for the safe and sound business plan.

Why Do Most of the Sales Leaders Fail to Build Their People?

The answer to this is quite simple, but not easy. It is one of the most complex mysteries, which always come to key features. Developing people and shaping their conduct is a whole new art that needs to be mastered to become a successful leader. In fact, it's not just art if you look at it from a different angle, it's a mixture of Art and Science since it involves a lot of calculations and precautionary measures.

You need to be very calculative and precise with your timings and decisions. The process is challenging yet productive. It's one of the most frustrating, tiring, exhilarating rollercoaster of emotions a person has to ride before landing safely onto the platform of success. And once you get all the notes correct, the reward will make your effort worth it as well as it will fill your wallets. To help your people grow and develop, you need to put them off the autopilot mode and direct their attention toward the technicalities of the job. Start training them on the areas where it is required. By doing so, you will be helping them learn something new and integrate further into the field.

Identify where your team is lacking and start training your employees to amend any flaws to produce their 100%. Maybe the lacking area is not so obvious in terms of detecting, you may need to conduct several tests and observe closely to identify where the person is lacking. The three most important groups in your business are: People (your customers), People (the managers) and People (The employees). All too often, business is placed in a category of interaction where people, society, and empathy do not matter.

To receive the desired outcomes, you need to make sure of the required inputs. To build people's ability to generate sales and reach the desired target, you may need to make some amendments with the inputs. Salespersons need to adopt three transformative and effective qualities:

- First and foremost, they need to manage their attitudes and get in control of their emotions. Day by day, moment by moment, staying determined of their goals. Being creative, and wanting to do what the business needs them to do.

- Secondly, they need to master the art of selling. Whether it is a transactional or a complex sale, every code can be cracked, maybe not so easily, but eventually. Science and art of selling must be integrated into one's thoughts and should be practiced enough that it gets infused in the employees' nature.

- Thirdly, they need to maintain a formal decorum through disciplined execution. For instance, doing the right thing at the right time and the right place accompanied by the right people. Staying focused and avoiding any distractions and temptations that may result in the causes of decline and time wasted.

Developing people requires you to acquire an interesting yet tough skill set. As a leader, you should enable others to be independent and direct their energies to produce better results. Help them focus and pay attention to their attitude, competence, and execution.

However, for the leaders and developers who fail to master this step of successful leadership, they pay a huge price for this failure. Disinterested salespersons, unclear and ineffective sales processes, demotivated labor, inability to identify the area where a person is lacking and providing specific training to fix the problem. All of these contribute to poor productivity and even lesser optimum sales results.

Leadership, or a successful leadership, to be precise, comprises numerous developing factors. For instance, having a safe and sound future, having a strategic approach, efficient processes, marketable product, or an incomparable service contribute to a successful business planning. However, for successful business planning along with effective leadership, it all comes down to the people associated with the organization. It all comes down to the people within the organization to execute the strategies, plans, and processes to make a business successful.

If we look at the boundaries and carry out an upper surface inspection, every organization and business understand this concept intellectually. Or do they? I believe partially yes, they do, that's why you often get to hear phrases like 'our employees are our most valuable assets' or 'our employees are our investments' and such cliché meaningless stanzas. However, when you look closely and have an insight of the inner operations, you get to know how employees are rather being treated, the authority they are given, or the level of trust and value they possess within the organization. You will realize the reality of the extent of this mantra, which is just a trite saying at many companies.

Customers will never love a company until the employees love it first

Simple, yet has a deep meaning. This evokes a sense of awareness and belonging within the company. Employees must go beyond their limits punching the time clock and collecting their paycheck. They need to bring that passion and motivation to bring that desired product to the table. They need to be empowered to do what's right on the customer's behalf.

Make your team a part of the process by informing them and discussing the whole plan with them. Do not just divide the workload in abrupt fragments to every individual and assemble it all chronologically at the end, while keeping all the credit. Make your team a part of the process and ultimately, making them a part of success. Give them credit for their efforts. Once you involve your team in this process, things begin to get much easier for you. You, as a leader, will be allowed to stay within your strengths and make a higher contribution, while making your team happy. Sadly, we have a culture of not promoting the 'Happy Team' or not even recognizing the term. We are more focused on meeting the deadlines, accomplishing the goals, long to-do lists, profitability, and workload. We do not even bother and for some leaders, it's not even considered as a necessary part of integral leadership. It is not a hidden fact; the internet is filled with results and statistical research that concludes the significance of happy team members. In all the cases, teams that were happy and satisfied with their work environment and workplace outperformed the teams that were not happy.

Focus on your team's satisfaction and happiness, and you will observe high output and more profit.

What is good people management and what effect does it have?

Highly engaged and devoted employees in the workplace are likely to contribute more to the company's success. This is due to their satisfaction which they receive in return from the management and work environment. They are usually willing to apply their skills above and beyond their caliber to accomplish tasks, which could help the organization achieve its goals.

Everyone loves to get considered and recognized for their work. Many researchers have shown that employees who considered themselves working for an effective leader scored twice better when it came to engagement assessment, as compared to those whose managers were incompetent. It is therefore a vital step to understand good management.

A 'good' manager is a title associated with a lot of responsibilities that fall under the category of managing and empowering the subordinates and employees. A good manager is expected to create a healthy work atmosphere and create an engaging, more effective work environment by empowering employees of their workforce. This aspect of business management links to the previously discussed aspect of finding the potential and putting it to use. Being in the managing position, an effective manager is supposed to keep the whole staff involved by keeping every member of the team on the same page and up to date with the new information. He is also entitled to treat each person as a unique individual and ask them what they personally want out of the company – utilizing their ideas to bring out that positive change. Leaders should not be blind to the problems their staff is experiencing. Two-way feedback is highly effective and essential in bringing out positive outcomes.

Good people management also accounts for practicing open, reciprocal communication, and investing in training for staff to reassure them that they have a promising future with the company. Of course, the behavior of managers should also always be consistent with the values of the organization. The last thing a person would like to deal with is an inconsistent unpredictable manager. An unpredictable leader has a negative impact on the productivity of an employee since they are always in constant tension and afraid of what is going to come next.

Appreciation and recognition work like magic in motivating employees. I cannot stress enough on this point, but recognition and being credited for the efforts brings about a positive change in his/her productivity. Those who feel like valued members of the team, and an instrumental component in achieving the company's success, tend to engage more in their work, thus they deliver the best. Employees begin to get a sense of loyalty and eventually begin to work exceptionally harder since they find their work personally satisfying and rewarding. As a business leader, you are bound to pay your team regardless of their productivity if their overall productivity yields result or not. Hence, to understand the 'people' factor in-depth, people management sheds light on the areas of actively disengaged people in the organization, and how to encourage them to work by directing their energy.

However, the beneficial outcomes and positive changes of good people management extend beyond bolstered efficiency. Such employees are satisfied with their managers and workplace, and they comparatively have more confidence in the organization's future and can therefore, be expected to stay with the business for a longer period. More importantly, conducting this development with your employees, you want to retain them at your company. This, in turn, is a great benefit for the employers as well.

People in Marketing Mix – The 4 P(s)

One of the most vital aspects of business growth happens through marketing. The marketing mix is the title given to the ingredients of a successful marketing strategy. 'People' is one of the most important integral parts of any successful marketing strategy. Without the people, who would buy your products or services? Without people who will manufacture and distribute your goods and services?

Most business leaders overlook the importance of this factor and neglect the idea completely. One of the facts behind this negligence is that not everyone is respectful of their customers. We have, many times, seen companies fail because of the people who are running them. It's due to their sheer negligence, wrong decision-making, and personal preferences over the work requirements.

How many times have you noticed restaurant staff being disrespectful and passively conveying their irritated mood onto their customers? A lot. What most leaders need to understand is that people are the most important part of the whole system. In fact, they are the backbone of the organization. Therefore, the management should ensure their employees are motivated enough to represent the organization positively. For example, let us look at a barbershop. If you do not get a proper haircut, you might never enter that shop again. Why? Because your needs were not satisfied, and your expectations were not met. This crucial step is where a business makes it or breaks it. The most successful companies put the right people in the right job. Thus, you can see how important people are becoming to the marketing mix especially if it is a small-sized business (especially for the entrepreneurs).

The value is not only felt in the development or manufacturing process, but also in the distribution and delivery sector as well. people have an important role in the distribution and service delivery sector as well. They are dependent on delivering and maintaining transactional marketing.

Develop the habit of thinking through both perspectives, being the observer and the decision-maker. Evaluate yourself where you need to work to improve your work environment as well as put yourself in the shoes of the consumer. What are their demands? Are their demands being met? To carry out successful leadership tasks, you need to think from the eyes of every person responsible for carrying out business operations including sales, marketing strategies, and other goals. Is not it odd that businesspeople and entrepreneurs spend a heavy fortune and invest a lot of their energy to think through every chunk of marketing strategies and marketing mix, and yet pay little attention to managing the individuals on their team. They fail to realize that for every specific job there is a person who is destined to be there due to his exclusively distinctive skills and qualities. No matter how big a fish is, it cannot climb a tree. Your very first decision of putting people in charge, hiring, recruiting, and appointing them to specific tasks, pretty much defines the progress your company is going to make. You need to get the right people on the bus, and then get them seated in the right places.

In most of the cases, you cannot proceed further unless you have placed the right people in the right positions. In today's date, many of the business plans are sitting on the shelves because their founders could not execute them successfully.

Problem Solving Is a Major Leadership Quality

People are the central part of any business organization and a vital element in bringing about an organizational change. Business strategies that focus only on the systems, process, and structures are bound to fail eventually. To boost employees' performance, managers need to work effectively on the grounds by engaging with their staff to execute successful and sustainable change. It is crucial for a company to periodically assess and improve management of people and leadership skills to boost employees' productivity. This, in turn, will grow your business.

Your people, as we discussed, already are your most important assets. Maybe not in terms of money, but in growth and assessment. You can compare the success of your product growth by determining the customer's experience. If the customer's experience was good, then in that case you succeed, if it's bad, you get a chance to learn and improve. When a customer complains because of one specific customer support executive, the customer is going to judge the reputation and quality of the whole organization by the service provided to him by the representative.

In that scenario, the customer support representative is the primary source of interaction, and the only bridge connecting the customer with the organization. The whole company is dependent on the customer support representative to build a valuable reputation and fulfill the client's requirements as well. Every staff member determines how stakeholders respond to the company in the market.

Here are a few things that you can carry out to improve your work environment and polish your leadership skills.

- **Have an evolved future vision with clear objectives:** A leader with a clear vision can lead his organization to achieve wonders. Envision your subordinates and employees into believing big. Always have a bird's eye view while planning and solving workplace problems.

- **Maintain effective communication with the audience:** Each staff member needs to be recognized and should know their worth. To expect the best possible desired outcomes, be sure you have conveyed the message effectively and provided all the required details. Also, all members of the organization clearly need to understand their role in delivering exceptional services.

• **Adopt an upside-down organizational view:** This strategy evokes a sense of responsibility and importance given to the people associated with your organization and product. For instance, prioritize your customer's needs at the top, then those who represent your company directly to the customers. Keep yourself on the bottom to be the top successful leader. The higher the designation, the more the responsibility.

• **Evaluate, identify, and implement:** Your company must identify and evaluate the customers' satisfaction level. Programs must be developed and implemented to ensure such practices in the company, which lead to more satisfaction of the customers.

• **These programs must incorporate measurement and feedback**: systems that continually monitor the "customer experience." Services at different levels between customers and managers must be improved with the focus on the mutual objective of superior services and maximize profits.

- **Motivate and give credit to your employees for their hard work:** Come up with motivational programs and schemes to keep your employees happy and engaged in their work. The happier and satisfied an employee is, the happier and satisfied your customer will be. Moreover, awareness programs regarding educating the staff and training-based sessions must be conducted occasionally to let the employees know what you expect of them in the new work environment.

However, **service delivery strategies cannot be built on foundations of sand**. The company must ensure its growth and adapt to the changing surroundings. Moreover, the company must continue developing and strengthening the structural underpinnings of its business.

Every leader must place emphasis on customer service as the means of maintaining the organization's position in a competitive saturated market. Having that said, the organization's service delivery model must evolve and improve the ways in which customers are supported. If a leader fails to execute this strategy, it can threaten the survival of the organization in the already thriving conditions.

Indeed, we must keep a track of and pay keen attention to the operations involving people, process, and technology. To create a successful corporate culture that defines success through the provision of efficient services, you must cater to the needs of the people (the customers and the employees).

Chapter 11
Approachability

"Power creates difference. Leaders bridge the gap."
Phil Wilson

Many companies these days are cursed with bosses who are not leaders. Leaders bridge the gap that power creates. An effective leadership calls for effective communication without any interruptions or barriers. An effective leader is a person who is approachable to his fellow associates, subordinates, and employees. As a leader, it is your responsibility to eradicate any existing barriers and to build the atmosphere for easy communication where anyone can come up to you and talk out the things that matter. Approachability keeps the channels of communication open and builds a healthy bond of trust between the employer and the employee. The previously conceived image of a strong leader is tough as a nail or deserted from the crowd or who is to be feared of, is outdated. The contemporary leadership calls for a person who is expressive verbally and nonverbally towards their employees. To execute a successful business plan and management strategy, building healthy, strong, and trustworthy relationships are essential. In this chapter, we will look at the factors and consequences impacting the approachability on leadership and productivity.

Approachability and high standards of professionalism are not mutually exclusive. They are, in fact, compliments. A difficult leader needs to put in a bit more effort to ensure they are open to their people's ideas. Doing so can make the difference between leaders enduring and achieving. Step out of your glass-walled building and try to effectively communicate with your associates.

Try to understand the needs and demands of every individual and build a strong bond with those reporting to you, within the boundaries of professionalism, fairness, and consistency. The better the bond you have, the better, more innovative, highly creative, and truly outstanding results you will observe in return from your team and subordinates.

Keeping a "Healthy-Distance" is Not an Effective Leadership Trait

First, when I talk about being approachable, we don't mean that you have to be everyone's 'buddy' at the workplace, this trait can weaken the leadership. When we talk about being approachable, we mean creating a comfortable environment where anyone and everyone can come up to you and share their problems with this confirmation of being heard in an organization. Employees who develop this understanding of being heard and recognized, perform exceptionally better than others. It creates a sense of familiarity toward the job and workplace and hence, increases the productivity level.

Most of the new leaders, or people new to the position, tend to intentionally maintain a distance from their subordinates for a few reasons. They are always delusional about their effective leadership traits, which keeps them dwelling between two personalities and they cannot be their own true self at the job. They are always overburdened by the thoughts of keeping the balance, for example, a leader might think if he or she becomes way too friendly with the subordinates, he might lose his respect and value in the eyes of his associates. Moreover, some leaders may tend to think being too approachable to their employees can be difficult for them in the future when faced with reporting bad news. Plus, if a leader gives more attention to one individual than the other, the rest of the team will think you are being biased toward that team member. The next thing you know, there is an atmospheric tension of favoritism and negativity that may arise amongst the team. Thus, we can conclude that leadership can be tough to balance, but it is not about just balance, it's about stabilizing the organization which is a much more difficult task than balancing.

The last thing an employee would want to experience at a workplace is an unpredictable boss. When you are less approachable, people have less idea about who you are. Your perception of them is totally dependent on what others have told you, which is completely biased. And the newcomers, especially the newcomers, who are highly motivated toward a new job and environment and high spirit of work, are highly affected by unpredictability. For such leaders, it is essential to understand that the workplace environment, effortlessly and naturally builds up required healthy tension.

An Effective Leader Draws People towards Them; the Leader-Team Bond

When you are approachable, your team members tend to talk to you more easily. They look up to you in problem-solving strategies and bring issues to you before they become a full-blown crisis. Team members who have approachable managers and bosses feel able to contribute more to the team and not just sit idly. They participate in group tasks as well as perform better individually. This participation is the consequence of the firm belief that employees have in the workplace and their leader. They are not scared about getting knocked off or humiliated at the hands of their organization for their valuable opinions. They know their leader is open to their suggestions and will consider them fairly.

However, your employees will hold back because of your unapproachable aura. Therefore, you, as a leader, may miss some great news influencing your organization and your position in the near future. The cost of not getting to know about the alerts and predictive alarming situations can make things worse and is certainly unavoidable.

And not just the professional life problems, build a bond with your subordinates where they can be open about their personal life problems to you as well. Maybe you can be of help to them, or maybe you can understand their mindset in that timeframe or what they are going through and assign them either the further tasks or holidays as per their needs. Knowing your employees' personal life builds a bond of trust and a healthy relationship. No, you do not have to intervene in someone's personal life until and unless they are willing to share it with you on their own. All that you need to do is make sure to create an environment where your employees feel comfortable to share their personal life problems with you. When you understand your employees at a personal level, they understand the organization better and take their jobs seriously.

When you can know your employee better and what he or she is going through in the new normal, you will be able to assess them and judge their quality of work. Surely, you do not want to risk a critical client with a coordinator who is already going through a crisis in his or her personal life. However, this does not indicate that it is your fault or the employee's, it is just that an effective leadership calls for better assessment and recognition of the potentials of the individuals. And as a leader, it is your duty to not just recognize what the other person is going through, but also help him or her get through it with your help, by any means possible. Most of the employees crave the recognition that they deserve, which they may unfortunately not get. If you can make your employees realize their worth and how important they are to the firm, they will get a sense of belonging and eventually, perform better at their job.

Approachability's Pragmatic Leadership Advantages

Never underestimate the power and positive outcomes of being approachable to your team and people you are dependent on to get your work done. When you are approachable, you understand people more, and the same goes for them. It develops a healthy bond where everyone is open to critiquing and sharing their innovative and creative ideas. They are ready to contribute to the cause, to make a noticeable difference. They understand what is needed for success and are willing to roll up their sleeves to get the work done.

For the leader and the team, knowing each other generates trust that leads to candor and ultimately, invites your people to share important information with you in a timely manner. Stand apart from your people and you will turn them off from doing their best consistently.

If your employees are hesitant to come up to you to discuss any noticeable difference that goes out of the pre-scripted pattern, either good or bad, you need to act on the situation to get the things on the right track. They might be holding onto some valuable information, which they think is not that considerate, but holds great value for the future predictability of the process. If you have experienced any one or two of such experiences, it is high time for you to reevaluate yourself and analyze where you may lack any of these effective leadership qualities. Are you approachable enough? Check yourself first, whether you are frustrated about the fact that you are not getting reports about the important withholding information on a timely basis, and if it is causing troubles for you to cope up with the problem-solving process due to lack of time. This helps to suspect your own proximity of approachability towards people. As a matter of fact, look out to some of the few trustworthy people you are close to, and ask them if they think you might put people off more than you know. Also, give them some space to be honest about the actual scenario and not just sugarcoat it for your sake.

If you discover you may have an approachability issue, here are a few suggestions to try out:

- When people speak to you about their problems, or provide you with the information, acknowledge it. Try to make it a habit at such moments to say some words of appreciation. Sometimes, just 'thank you for the updates' can brighten up the day of your employee.

- As a part of healthy reconciliation and deeper understanding, go a level deeper in getting to know your employee. Try to invest more time in them.

- Let your people know you a little bit better than just being a boss. Try to initiate a conversation or discussion that goes beyond the specific tasks and deliverables.

- Do not stay back when it comes to expressing emotional sentiments towards others. When it's heartfelt, don't hesitate or hold back. Emotional attachment of a leader to his subordinates has a huge impact on their productivity.

- Listen- you can emphasize active listening or listening to the sake of hearing and not only responding! I cannot stress enough on this point, 'the importance of being a good listener'. To understand, always listen first before you reply. Moreover, avoid any distractions such as indulging in other activities when people are talking to you – pay attention.

- 'I know' is ego, not leadership. Try to differentiate between your choices of diction. Moreover, welcome new ideas and suggestions from your team members.

- Consider making extra effort to be gentle with people who are easily intimidated, or less prone to go "toe to toe."

- Avoid overreacting to bad news. When you overreact to a certain situation, it embeds fear in the hearts of your subordinates, and they hesitate to come up to you to talk about the things that matter.

- Cut down on the sarcasm and be straight to the point. Your employees may often misinterpret your signals even if all you were trying was just being funny or lighten the mood.

- Be consistent. Employees who have bosses with dynamic mood swings tend to fear to share their ideas thinking they might set off the mood of their leaders or their leader may react in some certain tone. The fear of humiliation always resides in the nature of the employees with unpredictable bosses, and this fear is reflected upon their performance.

Putting the Right People in the Right Places

One of the most crucial tasks of leadership is to appoint people in the places where they can be the most effective. The person in the leading authority defines through his conduct how the team is going to perform collectively. If the leader is going to be demotivating or biased, you can expect worse outcomes from the team members.

When you promote someone, who lacks the required leadership qualities and people skills, you are not only setting that person up for failure as a leader but also drastically damaging the culture of your workplace. It is like planning for failure despite knowing all the possible outcomes. To be a leader, you do not have to be the highest achiever or highest performer. You need to possess certain skill sets and personality traits, which define good effective leadership. You can help promising leaders develop some of the key leadership skills mentioned above. However, if you care about your reputation as a leader, the best advice I can give you is to promote good leaders from the get-go. Trust me when I say it is not as easy as it may sound. You may receive some serious backlash in the popular opinion for selecting people based on their leadership qualities rather than their performances. You may even get to listen to phrases like being biased or buddy-buddy. You need to be vocal about what you feel about the people on your team.

Your decision might be unpopular at first but only you know that this will help you out in the future, and it is for the betterment and prosperity of the organization. The person, who you appoint for a certain position, maybe an average performer, but could possess great leadership qualities. As a result, this might upset the high performers of the team, which would demotivate the others. Therefore, you must have strong convictions about your decision and be able to clearly explain why you made the choice you did.

There are plenty of ways to develop, support, and show appreciation for those employees who are great at their jobs but missing some of the qualities of real leaders. Even if you are not looking to promote anyone right now, start looking for the leadership traits amongst your team members. When you spot someone doing one, let them know. People love feedback and noticing these traits will be especially gratifying. These are good prospects for future leadership roles. Proceeding further, we will talk in detail about some of the leadership aspects which will cover up the major parts of the understanding to be a better leader. Below mentioned are some of the key qualities and traits which you can practice and adapt to groom your personality as a more appealing leader and to create a positive impact on people's perception of you.

Be a Good Listener

If your team members think that you are not listening, they would not only stop talking, but they would also stop approaching you for any problem. Approachable leaders listen more than they speak. Be a listener who listens carefully, quietly, and without passing any judgments. Just keep listening and let the other person say what they want to say, even if their views are significantly different than yours. Active listening is not about continuously just sitting there with no expression and waiting for the other person to finish speaking so that you can have your two cents. "Always listening not to respond but to hear".

You don't have to worry about fixing things as a leader. Attentive listening is a key element, which promotes others to speak their understanding on the subject and come up with better possible solutions. The understanding you gain from listening in-depth helps your audience (your employees), as well as it helps broaden your horizons into new dimensions.

To engage in active listening, you must engage your eyes, ears, posture, and body language to express your full attention to draw on your emotional intelligence. Through active listening, you completely understand the message the other person is trying to deliver and as a result, you can draw better and valid conclusions.

Moreover, attentive listening helps you gain the trust of your employees. On the other hand, through empathic listening, you can get to the root of any issue your employees are dealing with. For instance, with the help of empathic listening and active listening, you show to the speaker that you are paying attention, which makes the speaker feel engaged and valued. This way they trust you with not just professional but personal matters as well.

Earning Their Trust

Trust is fundamental for effective leadership and successful organization. Trust goes both ways, from leaders to the employees and from employees to the leaders. Every day a leader asks the team members to walk into the unknown, and all the team members do as request. When your employees trust you, you are a successful leader.

The best way to start building trust is by bringing changes to your own behavior, which would help you to build a success-oriented relationship with your colleagues and staff.

Some of the behaviors you can practice upon and adopt in your personality to gain employees' trust are:

- Providing honest feedback, even when it is difficult. Just make sure to not to go too harsh when it is not necessary.
- Drawing conclusion on mutually agreed discussions
- Giving others the opportunity to fail
- Owning up to your mistakes

These are some of the things that you can work upon to gain the trust of your organization. A relationship based on mutual trust knows no bounds and once you have reached that level of mutual understanding with your employees, your company will achieve new heights of success.

Reach Out to Them as a Peer or a Friend

Set aside some time to spend with your team. People are drawn to those who share genuine care and concern for others. Ask your team members questions and try to initiate a conversation, which is not just related to the work and deadline or reports. Ask them about their personal life if they are willing to share. Ask them if they are encountering any barriers to work or ask them about the troubling factors and distraction from outside the work, avoid the political minefield we are in currently.

As an effective leader, simply asking 'how can I help your employees is the most powerful tool. Being the boss is not about just ordering and getting work done by the people. When you start reaching out to your employees as a peer rather than a boss, they will feel more connected to their job. Showing your employees that you care and that you are always there to offer a helping hand, makes it easier for them to come to you whenever they need help.

Similarly, seeking help is an attribute to great leadership traits. There are cases where some inexperienced leaders believe that leadership is all about getting their work done. However, great leadership is a lot more than this. Great leadership does not mean just taking the lead and never requiring assistance, in fact, it provides opportunities for others to shine, while simultaneously ensuring you get the best solution and the right person doing the job.

Making Sure Everyone Participates

Leadership is about bringing out the best in your employees. Employee empowerment does not just talk about achieving it but practicing it in your daily tasks. To achieve 100% results, you need to deliver 100% precise and accurate instructions. As a leader, you need to be proficient in your speech when you are assigning a task to your team members. Moreover, you need to ensure that everyone participates and that no employee feels left out in the organization. There are a lot of ways you can engage the whole team while directing them into collectively achieving success for themselves as well as the organization.

Eradicate solo-thinking by developing cross-functional teams that cut across departmental boundaries to take full advantage of the ideas and expertise of all your employees. When you assign employees to these teams, encourage them to take on both formal and informal leadership roles, and reward them when they do so. This practice will also lead to improved communication throughout your organization, greater ability to capitalize on opportunities, and coming up with effective solutions to difficult problems.

Nowadays, the most effective businesses encourage every employee to take on leadership roles. By doing so not only will it take some burden off the leader's shoulders, but even the employees will become happier, more engaged, and more efficient in your business.

Make yourself approachable as the governing trait of your leadership. Leaders who are approachable get things done, as they tend to develop supportive relationships with their subordinates.

Chapter 12
Honesty

"Honesty is the fastest way to prevent a mistake from turning into failure"
James Altuche

Honesty and transparency are some of the biggest attributes and qualities of an effective leader. In today's dynamic global environment, too often characterized by prominent examples of unethical practices and reality of increasingly frequent mergers, acquisitions and downsizing, followers' trust in their organizational leaders has become an important issue. As a leader, you should try to slim the walls of mere misconception between the management and non-management. The opacity grows as the veil thickens and to integrate transparency in an organization, a leader should work on thinning the veil.

Being transparent does not mean that you must exhibit every little confidential detail. It is more about avoiding or eliminating the already built culture of power differential and offering information that people need to know. Dual personality, whether intended or unintended, can create an atmosphere of workplace politics. You do not have to be a politician; you must be a leader. One important aspect of thinning the veil involves responding to the questions with utmost honesty, even if you think that is not the suitable option for the situation. For instance, if someone is asking for your attention and you reply with *"I'll get back to you,"* then make sure that you do or if you are replying *"I don't know,"* just make sure that you are unaware of the truth and possess no knowledge about the topic. Such as, if you tell someone that 'you are not at liberty to discuss' because it is confidential, stick to your words. Do not be a politician.

Transparency, as a value, is all about being open, honest, accessible, and approachable as a leader to your subordinates. The more transparency you have, the more people will trust and respect you. To develop a healthy work relationship and trust amongst the employees and the management, it is essential for a leader to be transparent in their conduct. Yet often leaders remove themselves from the teams they lead, focusing on communicating with the executive team and customers only, often neglecting the operational teams. The reasons for this separation are justified and there are as many advantages as disadvantages. Nevertheless, I believe that the most influential leaders are those that are visible and accessible to all.

Transparency Is the Key

Trust and transparency have become integral parts of any workplace as employees seek to be what is real and true. The last thing people want to expect from a workplace is an unpredictable environment and a boss with an unpredictable nature. People want to work in such an environment that allows them to have greater clarity of thought and promotes them to grow individually. The unpredictable environment in a workplace gives birth to delusional thoughts with each decision that we make or relationship we foster.

An employee wants to know from his/her leaders if the company is headed toward the right direction. They deserve transparency to protect themselves from any upcoming threats to their job. To be an effective leader, you need to trust people and gain their trust as well. One of the misunderstood perceptions that prevails in leadership is that most leaders think that if they become transparent, they will lose their dignity in the eyes of their subordinates. The thought of being less authoritative stops the leader from being vocal with their subordinates, which, in turn, makes them look less approachable. They believe that the credentials for which they have worked so hard to attain the position will make them lose their power, leverage, and dignity. As the scenario is changing, the demand and requirements for successful leadership are changing with the business demographics.

We are living in an era where people want and expect their leaders to be more of a human, less perfect, and at times a bit vulnerable, regardless of their hierarchy of rank. Employees like to work with a leader who shares a mutual intellectual level with them, a leader who is vocal about the problems, and a leader who discusses before jumping on to the conclusion.

"A man who trusts nobody is apt to be the kind of man nobody trusts."

HAROLD MACMILLAN

This way, employees feel familiar to the workplace and much more motivated, which is reflected through their performance. When an employee is given importance, consideration, and asked about his word in the matter, he feels a sense of familiarity with the job and the workplace. To run a well-functioning organization, it is imperative for a leader to communicate well to all employees of the organization. Through effective communication, the messages are processed and sent to the intended recipient at the time, as well as they are received and acted upon. It is incredibly important for a leader to be clear about the instructions he is delivering and what he wants in terms of an output from the subordinate. The losses are minimized if the instructions are delivered correctly, since there are fewer chances of things going against the instructions.

Many organizations, though, experience a breakdown in communication to some extent, and without being able to see where this breakdown is, it's hard to resolve it. If we speak in business context, communication openness has been defined as "message sending and receiving behaviors of superiors, subordinates, and peers with regard to the task, personal, and innovative topics."

What is Honesty?

A leader holds an important part in an employee's life; he or she can inspire them to greatness in life. Honesty is interlinked with the concept of positivity and integrity. Honesty is the ability to develop trust in followers and legitimacy. The actual definition of honesty in terms of leadership can be referred to as transparency and openness. Honesty is the measure of your willingness to communicate what you are thinking or feeling toward something even when it is uncomfortable, or the idea is considered unpopular.

Moreover, another important aspect related to honesty and leadership is that it is willingness to listen, sharing and discussing ideas before the data is completely thought through. When available alternatives are not completely crystallized or when the discussions are not final, this is the time when your consideration toward your employees, and how much their participation matters to you.

Within an organization, honesty can also be keeping your word, following through on promises, and delivering on time – which is an integral part of any successful and influential leadership.

If a leader would not be honest about his ideas and vision, how can he be truthful toward his subordinates or the people who consider him as a role model? As a leader, you are being observed all the time by your employees, managers, colleagues, subordinates, and others. You must lead by example by working on such important aspects of your personality, so that you can expect the same in return from your team.

What is Integrity?

Integrity in leadership is defined as the courage to speak up when your point of view is at odds with the general population. As a leader, it is not always true that people will agree with everything you say to them. In fact, there will be times when your opinion might not be that popular to the majority, but if it is beneficial in the name of the organization, you should do it.

A decision could be against the manager's perspective or with a commonly held belief about how things should be done in general. Integrity may also be interpreted as a work ethic. As a leader, you are at the top of the company, enjoying the aerial view. You can sense the problems before they arise and can prepare for them in advance to save the company from suffering any major losses. Even if that preparation holds you against the common belief amongst the organizations, you should still integrate it. Though the best option would always be to discuss the problems with the whole team.

What is Trust?

Trust is what keeps a relationship going and growing over time. Trust fuels the relationship and keeps it running smoothly. To run an organization smoothly, trust is practiced from both sides – management and non-management.

It is the first step toward building a healthy work relationship where people can share information regarding their ideas and can benefit the company through positive outcomes. For a leader, you need to be very certain about making sure that your company has faith in you. Every day your employees do the work you command them without asking you what it is about because of the faith they have in your goals and vision. In return, you should be more empathetic toward them and trust them with the work and decisions.

Trusting employees with special tasks evokes a sense of belonging and exclusivity in them – they feel more concerned and take more participation in the tasks. Moreover, in an effective leadership trust can be based on a feeling that you have the other person's back when he or she is not in the room.

It may be the confidence you will add on the other person's point of view with clarity and understanding. Or trust may be gained as you are seen to act in the best interest of the team or organization rather than acting primarily to advance your personal agenda.

Trust is a more complex term; it's not as simple as it may sound. It is one of the most critical attributes of a leader's personality. You can have a progressive vision, fail-proof strategy, excellent communication skills, innovative and creative ideas, and a professionally skilled team, but if people within or outside the organization don't trust you, you will never obtain the desired outcomes.

One of the biggest misconceptions, which leaders fail to understand is that trust does not come packaged along with the title of the leader or granted as an achievement. It is something that you have to work for and earn over a period of time through your excellent conduct and performance; it is more of a bond and relationship that you share with the people. Leaders who inspire trust, garner better output, morale, retention, innovation, loyalty, and revenue while mistrust fosters skepticism, frustration, low productivity, lost sales, and turnover. Trustworthiness amongst the organization affects the output significantly, thus, to obtain the desired outcomes, it should be the utmost priority of a leader to gain trust and become trustworthy for his team at the same time. Below mentioned are some of the qualities that a leader can work on to build trust:

- Demonstrate Passion
- Share your knowledge
- Keep Promises
- Entrust Your Employees with Special Tasks
- Effectively communicate
- Get to know your employees on a personal level
- Admit to your mistakes
- Be transparent
- Give them the credit

Influential leaders always follow up with these principles and align their conduct with such attributes, which distinguishes their behavior from the boss. Effective leaders draft the way and guide their employees, they produce a vision of upcoming missions. They inspire people, help others, and motivate their team members to be a better version of their own self. They set a strong example of their leadership traits such as honesty and integrity to inspire followers and other people associated with them.

Do What It Takes

Consider this fact that when you become a leader, somehow people already have a perception of you as being a dishonest person. A leader's utmost responsibility is to work on building a healthy relationship based on trust and honesty throughout the organization. The difference in perception makes it critical for a leader to identify what the managers, colleagues, reporting authorities, and other stakeholders are looking for when it comes to honesty, trust, and integrity. It has been identified through research that honesty in leadership has led to an increase in productivity as well as it has contributed to the increase in loyalty. If you want your employees to be honest with you, you need to be honest with them first. Honesty is contagious and works both ways, it is the first step towards building a healthy relationship. As for a leader, reaching out to employees and explaining the thoughts behind decisions is what transparency is all about. You show your employees why they are doing what they are being asked to do. You need to restore your faith in them to obtain an equal amount of trust from your employees. This practice can go as far as inspiring them to get behind your vision for the organization. Even if your employees disagree with you, explaining your thoughts will lead to a healthy discussion, which will yield positive results.

Mentioned below are some attributes of successful influential leaders, who lead their team and the organization they work for to the new heights of success by following a pattern of outstanding leadership qualities:

Model the Path

Great leaders are determined to explain values and goals honestly to their team members. Efficient delivery of instructions to the subordinates' results in expected outcomes. This process also eliminates the possible chances of any major losses from the employees. If the input is clear, the output will already be according to the expectations of the client. Honesty in instructions is not just about ordering subordinates to work, but it is also about owning up to the mistakes from either side. A leader should set a good example for others and inspire them for being honest.

Inspire a joint vision and aim

Honesty in leadership is reflected when a leader envisages a better future for his organization and followers. It is that innate quality in most influential leaders, which makes them consider themselves and their team as one unit. They realize the fact that 'it's their collective mission and not an individual task'.

A good leader listens and asks before making decisions. Moreover, they ensure their subordinates get a sense of belonging so that they can be involved in the process of decision-making as well as be able to share their valuable opinion. This sense of familiarity encourages an employee to perform better in his task, which raises the graph of his productivity.

Takes Challenges and Goes on Ventures

An effective leader is always keen to look forward to better opportunities and possibilities for his followers and organizations. This risk-taking quality is what motivates the employees to take challenges and face difficulties in difficult times. The leader would never fear from taking the risks in new experiments and stepping into new ventures for his team.

Inspire others to take the reign in their hands and act

Leaders collaborate with people's needs and mobilize their teams. Great leaders motivate their people and always encourage them to be the best version of themselves. They never stay back or retreat from empowering their team members.

Encourage people's efforts and appreciate them

One of the most highlighted qualities of an effective leader is that they never take all the credit for the completed tasks. An honest leader never claims credit for the work done, rather a leader recognizes, appreciates, and rewards the contributions along with celebrating the value and success. A smart leader will thank everyone on the team, instead of solely accepting the recognition for themselves. When employees know that you will thank them and credit them for the work, they get motivated and start working more efficiently as per demands. This mutual understanding develops a bond of trust and healthy relationship amongst the leader and his associates.

Admitting Their Mistakes

Although it can be pretty tough for some managers, bosses, and employees to come out and own up to their mistakes, however if you want others to be open to you, you should be open to them equally. If you let them know that making mistakes is human and this is the process of learning and growing, they will start trusting you.

If you want to be the best of the leaders, you need to acknowledge your error and normalize owning up to the mistakes in the organization. This way, you can receive honest feedback from your team.

Powerful Impact of Honesty – Things That Happen When a Leader Is Honest

Transparency is a powerful factor, which trails down to some of the major productivity outputs within an organization. When we talk about leaders being transparent in a workplace, we mean promoting one-to-one or direct interaction rather than the delivery of commands through third party interaction. Communicate less through e-mails and try to engage with your team members face-to-face as much as possible. Honesty yields positivity and productivity. Some of the major consequences when a leader is transparent are:

- Problem-solving becomes much more convenient and faster
- Teamwork – teams are built easier
- Relationships grow
- People begin to trust their leader and the organization they are working for
- Better performance is observed

Ask for feedback from your employees on how you have been doing as a boss and if there is anything you can do to make it better. Let them know that you are aware of your flaws and shortcomings, and hope for it to improve. This shows that you are willing and concerned about your team. This concern develops the trust amongst the team members, which results in benefits including increased innovation, collaboration, and improved quality. We are living in an era where people like to work with leaders who are more of a human and admit their mistakes. Relationships don't begin to shape until a problem is encountered and catered to resolve together. So, go first, take risks with openness and honesty, and encourage your team members to do the same.

Chapter 13
Your Mission Is Their Mission

"Every enterprise requires commitment to common goals and shared values."

Peter F. Drucker

Leadership is not a position; it is more of an action - a complete code of conduct. To run organizational operations smoothly, you need to align your thinking with your subordinates. The key principles and their alignment can help increase engagement and productivity in any organization.

When your actions begin to inspire others to dream more, learn more, do more and be better than yesterday, you become a leader. When you envision employees with what you perceive, employees understand the company's purpose and adopt it as their own. This practice, in every organizational process, aligns everyone's efforts and directs their energies into achieving the mutual goals together, as a team. People are the crux of every leadership effort. Leaders cannot lead until and unless they understand the people they are leading. One way to look at leadership is that the function of a leader is to lead and guide people who will follow with the same values. An effective leader, therefore, must be able to build relationships and create trust and honesty to lead the team toward a unified goal.

A Unified Goal

As business leaders, it is often assumed that the staff knows and understands what is going on within the company and that they understand the purpose behind the task. However, this is not always the case.

A collection of individuals with distinctive qualities working in various dimensions does not make up a good team. Nor do people who suddenly transform into a team merely because they work in the same organization. A true team, whose members work together by directing their minds, bodies, and energy in a singular dimension, has a unified vision. This vision enables any company to embark on any business ventures easily by having unity and faith within each other as well as in the organization and the management. Unity begins with the leader. You must be vivid in your vision and tactics in achieving the goal to bring the team together. Many organizations suffer because the people in leadership positions tend to have no clear vision, or maybe they have a vision but do not know how to execute? This ultimately creates a serious threat to the organizational structure and operations with people just following the rules without any proper instructions and lacking any clear sense of direction.

As a leader, you need to put the company's interest before your personal preferences and take actions accordingly. What sits at the core of any successful organization is its principles and values, which are important in guiding our priorities. True leadership calls for leaders and stakeholders working together, forming an alliance with the employees in achieving a mutual goal.

To rally a team around a common cause, you must have a clear vision, convey it to your team, and exhibit it creatively. What most people fail at is the second step regarding conveying the vision constantly considering that once they have delivered it, it is enough for everyone to understand. Moreover, such people lack at realizing the fact that not everyone in the organization shares the same level of familiarity or passion with your vision. Most leaders are constantly on the lookout for the next challenge and opportunity to grasp onto, thinking once they have communicated something, it has been understood and caught everyone's attention.

The Impacts of Unified Direction

Unity is the binding agent holding the team together. It does so by reducing competitiveness among its people. When people share a common goal, they work together with the mindset of complementing each other as a team instead of competing against one another. That is, they look for ways to make the other person do better instead of trying to outshine one another. Every person develops a sense that their performances can either improve or deteriorate the whole team's performance. This evokes a sense of familiarity and responsibility as each member of the team feels like he is being valued and trusted.

How Do Leaders Work Towards Goal Achievement?

One of the most crucial tasks of leadership development is to have the ability to influence your team member's leadership skills to meet the organization's demands. Leaders are bound to effectively guide how to achieve the goal, since team members' skills are necessary to yield desired outcomes. Revitalizing the spirit of teamwork and unified efforts is a much more complex task than it may sound. For an effective leader, it is imperative that his behavior should reflect on his conduct, influencing people to change. Although motivational factors and processes may vary across the organizations depending on the culture and nature of the task there are some leadership qualities present in every successful leader.

One of the greatest qualities of an effective leader, they push their employees to be better and lead effectively.

As a leader leading the group of individuals toward the main objective, there are some rules that apply to you. The goal as a leader, is to have the team members:

- Understand and then align their vision according to yours

- Take ownership of the vision
- Contribute to the vision
- Pass on the vision

"A team or leader with no vision will soon perish."
O'Neal Johnson Jr.

The team is said to be strong and cohesive if their leader possesses all the above-mentioned attributes in his personality. However, all too often we do not even take the first step of ensuring that the vision is understood. Test your team's unification around a common vision.

A mutually shared ideology or a unified vision increases the accountability amongst the team members, therefore making them dependent on each other for success. Through combined team efforts they mutually spur one another on to peak performance. This is what the main crux of leadership is, keeping the team's preferences over your own preferences.

At the same time, when a team is passionate about bringing its vision to reality, its members know immediately when someone gets off track. A healthy team confronts slackers and urges them to contribute to the team. This is healthy in a way because the weak link is identified earlier before it causes serious harm to the team.

A few leadership qualities that influence unified goal achievement include the ability to create a clear vision, the ability to understand *organizational culture*, the ability to focus on performance development, as well as the ability to encourage innovation. Some of the nodes that a leader can adopt in his career to help improve the team are listed below:

Make a Vision-Plan

Having a vision is fundamental; it lays the foundation for an organization to flourish for goal achievement. To provide a clear route or a directional compass for each contributor within the organization to follow, having a firm belief in your goals as well as spreading awareness about your plan is necessary. Depending on the level of leadership, many leaders are not responsible for creating the vision for the company but are responsible for:

- Articulating the vision
- Aligning team members to operational strategies

- Taking necessary measures by prioritizing the company's vision linked to the success

For instance, maximizing the profits is an objective which requires the engagement of the whole team. Leaders may indulge team members into productive activities that correlate to the fulfillment of revenue, growth, and organizational culture goals. Moreover, to improve the interaction between departments regarding organizational culture, team members may brainstorm some qualitative methods and strategies. This type of activity allows a team to focus on accomplishing departmental tasks that translate to the company's goals and vision.

Make your vision a part of the company's process

Whether its recruitment, training, or onboarding processes, make sure your employees are aware of the vision you behold from the first day. It is highly emphasized for an employee to understand the company's vision and get aligned with it. The idea or the vision should be incorporated through several techniques such as discussing during the training process, stressing more frequently into the onboarding process, and then bringing it up again and again consistently throughout the span of their employment period.

For the company's vision to be remembered and understood by all employees, it needs to be precise and relatable for every employee at every level to be able to interpret the essence through it. A few of the viable steps to make an effective vision statement are:

- **Define the company's output through clear instructions**: What is the outcome you want for your customers?

- **Define the Unique Twist** - What makes you different or special? What is your unique selling point that highlights your existence from others?

- **Apply Quantification** - How will you measure your progress along the way?

- **Add "Human" Aspects** - How can you make it relatable or tangible?

Create a vision from the inside out, not from the top down

As leaders or directors, it is your foremost professional responsibility to guide your team's vision and align every single employee's performance. It is extremely important for a leader to make sure all their employees are on the same page and they progress unanimously towards the same goal. But this does not mean that leaders should be solely responsible for the task of spreading awareness of the vision. In the case of a united team, awareness regarding the vision can come from the team members.

Hiring is a crucial step in any organizational process, which defines the success and the future profitability of the company. If you are making sound hiring decisions that consider factors which go beyond the task at hand, such as grit, empathy, and the drive to speak up, then you are filling your ranks with people who have a vision, and are good at identifying the goals of others as well

In an environment filled with visionaries, a leader's role is no longer to create and sustain a vision, but to nourish the different minds and help guide them toward a stronger, unified approach.

Tie your vision statement with the goals

To ensure that everyone is aware of the vision of the company, it should be tied to realistic goals for employees. By framing your vision in this manner, you are turning the company vision into an integral part of the daily experience.

Everybody on either side of the command, whether the CEO or an employee, should be feeding into the system to reach their goals which will, in turn, push the company toward its goal. By aligning your vision with goals, employees are inspired to hold each other accountable to be their best and contribute to the company's vision.

Lining up your employees' goals with the company's vision is a crucial aspect in having a successful company. Having the right <u>Employee Performance Management software</u> tools and infrastructure to help create this alignment is also imperative. Ensuring that everything is in place to support these processes is of the utmost importance for an organization's growth.

"Individual Performance Planning and Assessments are acutely positioned to manage employee's development."
O'Neal Johnson Jr.

Clear and effective communication

For effective leadership, one of the most vital strategies that must be put into practice at every organization is to prioritize concise and clear communication across the board. There should be no communication gap between the chains of commands. To achieve the desired outputs, it is incredibly important to deliver clear instructions, so that you can be sure that the team members will invest their full efforts.

People are bombarded with messages every day, creating saturation amongst the team. Your mission is to make your organization's message stand out to employees. It may seem like a challenge to make this message matter to the team members, but it only seems that way because the answer is so simple: communicate it. Companies often overcomplicate their communicating channels by tangling them with the official formalities.

Your vision and its delivery should be simple, not simplistic. To ensure employees get the message about your organization, make its purpose, mission statement or manifesto simple and easy to understand. The company's goals and objectives associated with the vision must be conveyed through reliable and comprehensive methods.

Emphasize the importance of working unanimously towards achieving a goal. Make sure your employees understand how working towards their goal is aligned with the company's vision and success.

In addition to comprehensive methodologies and effective ways of communication, face-to-face or one-on-one communication with the employees regarding the vision of the company usually leads to an increase in the company's profit. Moreover, a company should and must take the advantages of modern technological advancements such as texts, blogs, emails, and other such communication platforms. Display your vision prominently in as many places as you can so that your employees see it often and can refer to it when needed.

Follow-Ups and Two-Way Feedback

With the continuously changing scenario, companies need to pick up their pace to keep up with the demand. In such dynamic circumstances, it would be highly efficient to ensure that there is two-way feedback between the employees as well as the authorities. To keep up with this competitive situation, a leader must take measures to make sure that the operations are running smoothly. It is highly unlikely for an employee to be only at the wrong since a leader is also a human being and can make mistakes intentionally or unintentionally. Moreover, it is also possible that a leader may be unaware of some important situation lingering around the organization, which can lead to major structural losses to the organization. It is important for a leader to be aware of any problem, and that the leader should have a contingency plan prepared to tackle the problem.

Oftentimes, weekly, or monthly check-ins will help your employees feel motivated and supported. Therefore, check in on their deadlines and projects, and support your employees' progress towards their goals, which should be aligned with the company's vision. When an employee is asked about his feedback as well as his opinion on any important matter, he gets the sense of belonging. This sense of belonging leads to higher levels of productivity. Moreover, to keep the cycle continuous, appreciate the feedback you receive from your subordinates. Recognize and reward team members who consistently accomplish their tasks on time and give reminders for improvement as needed.

Chapter 14
Leadership Styles

Which Type of Leader Are You?

Leadership style is the way a person uses their authority to lead, manage, and guide other people. There are a lot of leadership styles identified by the researchers, each one targeted for specific audience, followers, leaders, workplace, and situation. Furthermore, a certain situation helps determine the most effective style of interactions. Sometimes leaders must handle problems that require immediate solutions without consulting their followers.

There is no such thing as a one-size-fits-all-leadership style for every organization. All companies operate in different work environments and it is often seen that certain traits, which are effective in one place, are not that useful to others. However, having a thorough understanding of various leadership styles enables senior executives to not only adopt the correct characteristics for themselves, but also choose better managers throughout the organization.

We will cover a list of 12 different types of leadership styles below. You need to understand that not each of them is going to suit your way of leading or the operational conditions of your workplace, but will be helpful for your better understanding:

Autocratic Leadership

Autocratic leadership calls for the major authority and power the leader retains. Although this may sound a bit rude or against your expectations, however autocratic leaders have significant control over the staff and rarely consider workers' suggestions. This leadership style is solely centered on the boss or the ruling authority, with him holding all the power and responsibility.

In this leadership, the decision-making task is solely confined to the leader and not to the subordinates. A leader makes the decision by considering all the affecting factors, and then reaches out to the subordinates to communicate the idea with them. These leaders then expect prompt implementation on the decisions made by them. In this type of leadership, guidelines, procedures, and policies are all-natural additions of an autocratic leader. Statistically, there are very few situations that can support autocratic leadership. This type of leadership has little to no flexibility. Thus, this type of leadership style is not highly supported nor adopted by many leaders, but it can be necessary in some places such as the military. This type of leadership style is most suitable where jobs require extremely limited skills. One noticeable drawback of this type of leadership style is that it can kill creativity due to strict instructions of sticking to the strategy.

Democratic Leadership

Democratic leadership is also referred to as participative leadership. Its definition is pretty much evident from the name itself. Democratic leadership means a leader takes an input from the team either collectively or individually, before jumping on to any conclusions. It is the total opposite of autocratic leadership and is centered on subordinates' contribution of suggestions and opinions. Although a democratic leader delegates authority to other people who determine work projects, the responsibility is all his own. One of the biggest highlights of this leadership style is that there is two-way communication, from the top management to the lower level employees. Democratic leadership entails fairness, courage, intelligence, creativity, honesty, transparency as well as competence. Reportedly, high levels of performance and job satisfaction have been observed in this style of leadership. A company can benefit in these environments since the customer satisfaction level also increases. According to the statistics, it is one of the most preferred styles of leadership.

One of the drawbacks for this leadership is that the decision-making process is slow. This type of leadership might not perform well where there is a need for quick decision-making.

Strategic Leadership

Strategic leaders sit at the intersection between the company's main operations and its growth opportunities. He accepts the burden of executive interests, while ensuring that current working conditions remain stable for everyone else.

The strategic leader is geared to a higher proportion of the audience, who plans on creating an effective team or an organization and is not exclusive to only top hierarchy levels of the organization.

This type of leader has a distinctive operating style with most of its basis revolving around strategic thinking, which supports multiple types of employees at once. A strategic leader bridges the gap between the need for new possibility and practicality by providing a vision with a set of specific habits. Effective strategic leadership is what an organization and its members expect from a leader in times of change.

However, strategic leaders may set high expectations, since it is not essential for a leader to always make decisions that are sound to everyone.

Transformational Leadership

Just as the name suggests, transformational leadership is always transforming and improvising on the company's conventions. Unlike other leadership styles, transformational leadership calls for bringing change in organizations, groups, teams, oneself, and others as well. It is likely that the employees may have a specific set of tasks or targets to be achieved every day, however the leader would always force them to go out of their ways and achieve more.

Transformational leaders motivate others to do more than they are already doing and will always try to set the mark high for the employees to achieve. This type of leadership typically yields higher performance levels. Transformational leaders inspire their staff and employees through effective communication, and by creating an environment of intellectual stimulation.

This type of leadership style motivates employees to see what they are capable of and is highly effective amongst the growing companies. Transformational leaders tend to have more committed, concerned, loyal, and satisfied followers.

However, this type of leadership can be harmful at times as these individuals are often 'over-estimating-thinkers' who may require a more detailed and oriented person to successfully implement their strategic visions.

Team Leadership

Team leadership is all about working with the minds and hearts of the people involved. This type of leadership provides a strong sense of devotion by dictating the vision and vivid picture of the future, where it is heading, and what it will stand for.

The most challenging aspect of this leadership is whether it will succeed. According to the Harvard Business Review, team leadership may fail because of poor leadership qualities.

Cross-Cultural Leadership

This form of leadership deals with the situation in which there are various cultures in the society. This leadership has also industrialized to recognize front-runners who work in the contemporary globalized market.

With the high pace society, we are living in, there are people from every race and culture working with us from different regions and countries. You may also consider outsourcing when your company needs it, which is also another aspect of expanding into a new dimension and a new culture.

Organizations, particularly international ones, require leaders who can effectively adjust their leadership to work in different environments. Most of the leadership styles observed in the cosmopolitan cities and states are cross-cultural since people over there belong to different cultures.

Facilitative Leadership

Facilitative leadership calls for forming a synergistic alliance between the two stages of processes. Facilitative leadership is too dependent on measurements and outcomes. The effectiveness of a group is related to the efficacy of its process. If the group is highly functioning, the facilitative leader uses a light hand on the process.

As the name suggests, the facilitative leader provides or facilitates the organization and its team members with a specific set of rules and guidelines and helps them out in times of need – 'getting his own hands dirty with the team members'. If the group is not functioning enough, the facilitative leader will be more directive in helping the group run its process. An effective facilitative leadership involves monitoring group dynamics, offering process suggestions, and interventions to help the group stay on track.

Laissez-faire Leadership

'Laissez-faire', a French term, literally translates to 'let them do'. This leadership calls for giving a free hand to your employees with minimal or almost no interference. This leadership revolves around the concept of least power to the leader and greater authority to the employees. This can be viable in workplaces that require creativity as well as employees' input.

Although laissez-faire leadership can empower employees by trusting them to work in any way they like, however, it can limit their development and overlook critical company growth opportunities. Therefore, it is important that this leadership style is kept in check.

But within its characteristics, it is also found to be very ineffective in the aspect of leadership and management.

Transactional Leadership

This is a leadership that maintains or continues the status quo. Transactional leadership involves an exchange process, whereby followers get immediate, tangible rewards for carrying out the leader's orders. Transactional leadership can sound rather basic, with its focus on the exchange.

Transactional leadership behaviors include:

- Clarifying the performance expected from the followers
- Explaining how to meet such expectations

- Allocating rewards that are contingent on meeting the objectives.

Transactional leaders are common nowadays. These managers reward their employees for precisely the work they do. A marketing team that receives a scheduled bonus for helping generate a certain number of leads by the end of the quarter is a common example of transactional leadership.

Transactional leadership helps establish roles and responsibilities for each employee, but it can also encourage bare-minimum work if employees know how much their effort is worth all the time. This leadership style can use incentive programs to motivate employees, however they should be consistent with the company's goals, and used in addition to *unscheduled* gestures of appreciation.

While this can be an effective way of completing short-term tasks, employees are unlikely to reach their full creative potential in such conditions.

Coaching Leadership

Coaching leadership is all about 'coaching' employees to help achieve their goals as well as their targets. It involves teaching, coaching, and guiding followers to meet up with the expectations and the demands. It is like a push, which is provided by the leader to the followers to direct their energy and efforts in the right direction. Coaching leadership is highly effective as its results are reflected in the employees' performance. Through coaching leadership, a leader can ensure guaranteed success from his team since the guidelines, information, and the training being provided meet the required performance criteria. Coaching leadership does the following:

- Motivates followers
- Inspires followers (either by leading as an example or guiding a specific task)
- Encourages followers (through appreciation or rewards/incentives)

Charismatic Leadership

Charismatic leadership overlaps with the transformational leadership, as it is a quality which is hard to pin down but attracts followers and inspires them to perform or act. Charisma does not imply sheer behavioral change, but it involves the transformation of the followers' values and beliefs.

Charismatic leadership relies heavily on the personality and charm of the leader in question. Since the success of projects and processes is highly dependent on the leader's presence for initiation, it is not suitable for all leadership styles.

The company and the team are highly affected if a charismatic leader leaves, since his influence is strong, and people feel more comfortable in operating under his leadership. Moreover, the confidence and personality traits they develop or build within the members of the team over the time remain there within them for a long while.

Some of the key characteristics of charismatic leadership are:

- Communication
- Maturity
- Humility
- Compassion
- Substance
- Confidence
- Body language (positive)

- Listening skills
- Self-monitoring
- Self-improvement

Visionary Leadership

Visionary leaders are driven and inspired by what a company can become and achieve. Visionary leaders behold a perception and align their team members with it. They see beyond the ambiguity and challenges, and target for the better and higher results.

Visionary leaders inspire other followers and manage to bring all the people on the same page. One of the characteristics of an effective visionary leader is that he can create cohesiveness amongst the team members. Visionary leaders are highly devoted and determined on their goals and serve as confident coaches guiding the organization through transitions or difficult organizational areas.

Visionary leaders focus on the progress of the organization and tend to work on the bigger picture for the better tomorrow by learning from the current situation. They fuel the organization's success to the next level through inspiration. It is highly imperative for a leader to hold a vision to qualify as a successful leader since it is one of the key qualities. This form of leadership involves leaders who recognize that the methods, steps, and processes of leadership are all obtained with and through people. They translate the organization's vision into realities by inspiring their followers.

Below mentioned are a few of the traits of a visionary leader:

- Resilience
- Strategic Thinking
- Favorable toward innovation
- Skilled communicators
- Expert organizers
- Focused and enthusiastic
- Intelligent risk takers
- Open minded
- Imaginative
- Creative

- Persistent
- Collaborative

"Great leaders are almost always great simplifiers, who can cut through argument, debate and doubt, to offer a solution everybody can understand."

Colin Powell

O'NEAL JOHNSON JR.

Determine your leadership style - DISC Personality Test

D	I
S	C

UNDERSTANDING YOURSELF (DISC)

Circle only one word in each row that you feel describes you best right now. Then transfer your answers over to the Scoring Sheet. Total up each column. Your highest score is your predominate personality type.

#	A	B	C	D
1.	Restrained	Forceful	Careful	Expressive
2.	Pioneering	Correct	Exciting	Satisfied
3.	Willing	Animated	Bold	Precise
4.	Argumentative	Doubting	Indecisive	Unpredictable
5.	Respectful	Out-Going	Patient	Daring
6.	Persuasive	Self-reliant	Logical	Gentle
7.	Cautious	Even-tempered	Decisive	Life-of-the-party
8.	Popular	Assertive	Perfectionist	Generous
9.	Colorful	Modest	Easy-going	Unyielding
10.	Systematic	Optimistic	Persistent	Accommodating
11.	Relentless	Humble	Neighborly	Talkative
12.	Friendly	Observant	Playful	Strong-willed
13.	Charming	Adventurous	Disciplined	Deliberate
14.	Restrained	Steady	Aggressive	Attractive
15.	Enthusiastic	Analytical	Sympathetic	Determined
16.	Commanding	Impulsive	Slow-paced	Critical
17.	Consistent	Force-of-character	Lively	Laid-back
18	Influential	Kind	Independent	Orderly
19.	Idealistic	Popular	Pleasant	Out-spoken
20.	Impatient	Serious	Procrastinator	Emotional
21.	Competitive	Spontaneous	Loyal	Thoughtful
22.	Self-sacrificing	Considerate	Convincing	Courageous
23.	Dependent	Flighty	Stoic	Pushy
24	Tolerant	Conventional	Stimulating	Directing

LEADERSHIP DEVELOPMENT STEP BY STEP

D-I-S-C SCORING SHEET

DISC PROFILE	D	I	S	C
1.	B	D	A	C
2.	A	C	D	B
3.	C	B	A	D
4.	A	D	C	B
5.	D	B	C	A
6.	B	A	D	C
7.	C	D	B	A
8.	B	A	D	C
9.	D	A	C	B
10.	C	B	D	A
11.	A	D	C	B
12.	D	C	A	B
13.	B	A	D	C
14.	C	D	B	A
15.	D	A	C	B
16.	A	B	C	D
17.	B	C	D	A
18.	C	A	B	D
19.	D	B	C	A
20.	A	D	C	B
21.	A	B	C	D
22.	D	C	B	A
23.	D	B	A	C
24.	D	C	A	B
COLUMN TOTALS				

Chapter 15
Conclusion

"A true leader has the confidence to stand alone, the courage to make tough decisions, and the compassion to listen to the needs of others. He does not set out to be a leader but becomes one by the equality of his actions and the integrity of his intent."

Douglas MacArthur

The greatest of all leaders is the one who creates not just followers, but more leaders. It would be difficult to set a specific criterion to qualify for the best leader, since many theories conflict with each other. The best leader is the one who acts accordingly depending on the circumstances and the nature of work. The title of a 'leader' is not given, rather it is earned through moral values

Leadership is not just a single term or a title, it is a code of conduct with a set of rules to be followed and acted upon. The crux of leadership relies on treating people in your surroundings, from your fellow authorities to subordinates, every single person on any step of the chain of command.

However, to be a successful leader you need to possess a few moral qualities. These qualities, attributes, and traits should reflect in each aspect of your personality and business dealing. It is the conduct that defines your personality and shapes you as a leader.

> *"Leadership is a potent combination of strategy and character. But if you must be without one, be without the strategy."*
> **Norman Schwarzkopf**

Leadership is the ability to translate your goals into visions. Being a leader is not an easy role; you cannot please everyone all the time and will not meet everyone's expectations. A lot of responsibilities lie within the role of leader. An influential leader is the one who has the guts to speak and act against popular opinion. They lead their team by example, by indicating the path and necessary steps.

As a leader you will encounter various types of situations and emotions; there will be good times, stressful times, and even terrible times. However, a great leader is always able to lead a team to success, regardless of the situation that they are facing. Fortunately, you can put history on your side and use the lessons from others to develop admirable leadership strengths. There are a lot of qualities, responsibilities, and traits that go behind in the development of a great leadership. Let us have a little recap of what we have discussed throughout the book to strengthen your beliefs and traits as a leader. Below mentioned are some of the key qualities that every (successful) leader should possess and learn from to achieve better results for the company as well as to enhance his leadership skills:

Honesty and Integrity

Do you have honesty and integrity traits? They are two of the most important building blocks of a great leadership. How can you expect from your employees to be true to you when you are yourself setting the wrong example? Your company and employees reflect your conduct. By setting ethical values and moral responsibilities as key-values, you can reach new heights of success. Leaders succeed when they stick to their values and core beliefs, and without ethics, this will not be possible.

"With integrity, you have nothing to fear, since you have nothing to hide. With integrity, you will do the right thing, so you will have no guilt."
Zig Ziglar

Trust Building

Are you trustworthy? One of the biggest misconceptions, which leaders fail to understand, is that trust does not come packaged along with the title of the leader or granted as an achievement. It is something that you must work for and earn over a period through your excellent conduct and performance. Trust is more of a bond and relationship that you share with the people. Leaders who inspire trust garner better output, morale, retention, innovation, loyalty, and revenue while mistrust fosters skepticism, frustration, low productivity, lost sales, and turnover.

Trustworthiness amongst the organization affects the output significantly, thus, to obtain the desired outcomes, it should be the utmost priority of a leader to gain the trust of his team.

Below mentioned are some of the aspects that a leader can work on to gain trust from his employees and develop a bond of transparency and openness with them:

- Demonstrate passion
- Share your knowledge
- Keep promises
- Entrust your employees with special tasks
- Communicate effectively
- Get to know your employees on a personal level
- Admit to your mistakes
- Be transparent
- Give them the credit
- Joking or levity should work both ways
- Confidentiality always between yourself and your employees

Commitment

Do you have what it takes to be a committed leader? You must have heard this a lot of times in your life that great leaders lead by example. The essence of this saying revolves around the concept of commitment and devotion towards work. Your employees always look up to you as an example to know how to get things done. Nothing shouts commitment more than getting your own hands dirty with the rest of your employees to carry out a task. By being committed to the company and especially to your team, you will not only get the operation running smoothly, in fact you will earn the respect of your fellow team members. This way you will be able to instill that same hardworking drive among your staff.

To receive their maximum performance in every task, you need to put in your 100% to set an example for your teammates to follow. If your employees feel that you are lacking commitment or passion for the job, they will loosen up the pace, affect their performance. As a leader, your commitment and enthusiasm towards the tasks set an example for everyone to follow, as well as they help develop loyalty and respect for you from your employees.

Decision Making and Accountability

Do you make thoughtful decisions? Are you accountable to yourself and others? With great powers, come greater responsibilities. A good leader takes responsibility for everyone's performance whether good or bad. When things are going smooth and managed, a leader appreciates it and gives full credits to the deserving candidate. One of the greatest qualities of effective leaders is that they never take full credits for the work and always reward their employees and team members with appreciation. However, if things are not going well, a leader carries out a brief feasibility test, identifies the problem, and then looks for the solutions to cultivate the cause from its root.

> *"A good leader takes little more than his share of the blame and little less than his share of the credit."*
> ***Arnold H Glasow***

A leader's decision-making ability matters a lot to the masses, the right decision taken at the right timing pretty much speaks for the end results. A leader should think long and hard enough before jumping to any conclusion. Moreover, a leader should and must account all the possible influencing factors before making any decisions. But once the decision has been made, you should and must stand by it. This idea brings us to another major quality that a leader should possess, which is to make sure everyone is on the same page. Although, most of the time, leaders take decisions on their own because they know better about the surroundings as well as what goes beyond them. However, it is highly advised that you must consult the stakeholders before taking any decisions. After all, they will be the ones to get influenced by the positive or negative results of your decision.

Inspire Others

Can you inspire others? As a leader, you must understand that you are constantly under observation of your team members and that they are learning from your gestures, whether good or bad. You serve them as an example to follow to know how to perform ideally in the workplace.

When processes get tough, your team members or subordinates look up to you as an example to follow and guide them through the whole process. Persuading others is one of the most difficult tasks a leader must do. It can only be possible if you inspire your followers by setting a good example.

As a leader, you should always ***think positive*** and develop the same positive approach. Being positive in a negative situation is what leadership is all about. It is not like that you are running away from the situation or have closed your eyes and ears to the surroundings. Optimistic thinkers are great leaders as they hold a vision. They look for the good in every situation and in every person. They do not quit nor give up on the situation. They set their goals and keep trying until they have reached them. ***Optimistic leaders*** are clear about which direction they are taking their team towards, and what they would have to do to get there. They never experience 'failures', they experience 'lessons', and then learn from those lessons to avoid making the same mistake in the future.

Effective Communication

Do you communicate effectively? It is highly imperative for the information to be delivered correctly, every bit of it, to get the desired results. Communication plays a vital role in shaping leadership. Until you clearly communicate your vision to your team members and tell them the strategy to achieve the goal, you will not be able to get the results that you wanted to obtain. Communication opens the doors of transparency in the organization and helps develop the work relationship between the employees and leaders as well as the whole team.

"The art of communication is the language of leadership."
James Humes

Words have the power to motivate people and make them do the impossible. If you use them effectively, you can also achieve better results. Communication should be consistent when it comes to establishing work expectations or giving constructive feedback. With great communication, your employees will have a broad understanding of what they are working for. Moreover, effective communication calls for effective listening as well as being ***approachable*** to your employees.

When you are approachable, your employees tend to share their thoughts and opinions with you. By becoming approachable, it helps develop the bond of trust and empathy, which is particularly important for a leader to understand. Unfortunately, most leaders follow a dictatorial style and neglect empathy altogether. Due to this, they fail to make a closer connection with their followers.

If you want to communicate effectively and efficiently, do not be out of your employees' sight. Do not be known as the leader who communicates via emails only. Show up in person, as often as possible.

Creativity and Innovation

Do you always accept creativity and innovation? To keep up with modern advancements in the competing market, a leader must be creative and welcoming to new ideas. He must think out of the box and value his employees' opinions to evaluate it, and then act upon them to get ahead of the competitors. As a good leader is someone the team could look up to for answers or solutions, it is up to you to think outside the box when any issues arise.

"Innovation distinguishes between a leader and a follower."
Steve Jobs

Creative thinking and constant innovation are what make you and your team stand out from the crowd. Think out of the box to come up with unique ideas and turn those ideas and goals into reality. To set a mark in the world of leadership, a leader must possess all the above-mentioned qualities. Lacking any of these qualities would have a significant impact on your conduct as well as on your performance. You need to set an example to be followed by others. That is where your commitment, passion, empathy, honesty, and integrity come into play. Good communication skills and decision-making capabilities also play a vital role in the success and failure of a leader. Lastly, innovation, creative thinking, and having a futuristic vision are some of the key traits, which make a leader stand out.

O'NEAL JOHNSON JR.